Our Colonial Period

The Making of America

Our Colonial Period

The Chronicle of American History
from 1607 to 1770

A Bluewood Book

THE MAKING OF AMERICA

THE MAKING OF AMERICA:
OUR COLONIAL PERIOD

A Bluewood Book
Copyright © 1996 Bluewood Books

This edition produced and published in 1996 by
Bluewood Books,
a division of The Siyeh Group, Inc.
P.O. Box 689
San Mateo, CA 94401

ISBN 0-912517-20-4

Printed in USA

Designed and Edited by Bill Yenne

Also in the *Making of America* Series:
Exploration & Discovery (1492-1606)

Other titles of interest from
Bluewood Books:

100 Events That Shaped World History
100 Inventions That Shaped World History
100 Women Who Shaped World History
100 Men Who Shaped World History
100 Athletes Who Shaped Sports History
100 Folk Heroes Who Shaped World History
100 African-Americans Who Shaped American History
100 Great Cities of World History
100 Natural Wonders of the World

TABLE OF CONTENTS

A FOOTHOLD IN THE NEW WORLD

These efforts at navigation were soon joined by efforts at exploitation. After gold was discovered, the European conception of the New World went from being that of an obstacle to being that of a resource. The Spanish were lucky in that they found gold, and their outposts were set up largely to ship it back to their homeland. The English and French found little gold, but they began exploiting the abundant supply of beaver for their luxurious fur.

By the end of the sixteenth century, Europeans began to conceive of the New World as not so much a place to avoid or exploit, but as a place to put down roots and *live*.

With this, serious attempts at colonization began. North America was a harsh environment, and the earliest English and French attempts at colonization failed disastrously. Yet the people persisted, and by the beginning of the seventeenth century, permanent settlements began to take root. In the two centuries after Columbus opened Europe's eyes to the existence of the Western Hemisphere, the great powers established their dominions. The Spanish took control of everything south of what is now the United States, except Brazil, which came under Portuguese rule. England claimed the eastern

ENGLISH ADVENTURER CAPTAIN JOHN SMITH

part of what is now the United States, and the French dominated all the land to the north and west of the English.

In 1607, England finally planted the seed that evolved into the largest English-speaking nation in the world. Captain John Smith (1579?-1631) founded his settlement at Jamestown (named for King James I) in the territory of Virginia. The colony nearly failed several times, but the colonists held on, and in 1619 the people of Jamestown inaugurated the first representative assembly in North America, a precursor to the form of government that would later predominate.

It was in 1620 that another group of British subjects, who called themselves the Pilgrims, established another settlement at Plymouth 1620 in what is now Massachusetts. Fleeing what they perceived as political persecution of their religious sect, the Pilgrims came to America in their ship the *Mayflower* to establish a colony where they could worship as they wished without governmental interference.

Plymouth was to be important because it was the first successful North American settlement founded by ordinary Europeans without a charter from a European government.

Over the course of the next 300 years, what began with a small band of determined settlers at Jamestown and Plymouth became the most powerful political and economic power in the world.

NEW SETTLERS ARRIVING IN JAMESTOWN, VIRGINIA'S FIRST PERMANENT SETTLEMENT.

THE JAMESTOWN COLONY

King James I (1566-1625), the first monarch of the House of Stuart, came to the throne of England in 1603. High on his list of priorities was the project of colonizing his American possessions. In April 1606, he issued two patents to men of his kingdom that authorized them to possess and colonize that portion of North America lying between the 34th and 45th parallels of latitude.

Geographically, this territory extended from the Cape Fear River in present North Carolina to Passamaquoddy Bay between what are now Maine and New Brunswick. The first patent was directed to nobles, gentlemen and merchants residing in London. Their corporation was called the London Company and its primary motivation was colonization and commerce. The second patent was granted to a like body of men who comprised the Plymouth Company, which was located in Plymouth, a seaport on the southwestern coast of England. In the division of territory between the two corporations, the country between the 34th and 38th parallels was assigned to the London Company, and that between the 41st and 45th parallels to the Plymouth Company. The narrow belt between the two would be shared equally, but under the restriction that no settlement of one party should be made within 100 miles of the nearest settlement of the other.

The leader in organizing the London Company was Bartholomew Gosnold, with his principal associates being Edward Winfield, a rich merchant; Robert Hunt, a clergyman; and Captain John Smith, a soldier of fortune and a man of genius. Others who aided the enterprise were Sir John Popham, the Chief Justice of England; Richard Hakluyt, a historian; and Sir Ferdinand Gorges.

In governing the colony, the royal prerogative was carefully guarded. There was to be a Superior Council resident in England, with its members chosen by the King. An Inferior Council living in the colony was provided for, but the members of this body were also to be selected by the royal authority and might be removed at the pleasure of the King. All the elements of government were reserved and vested in the monarch.

Paternalism was carried to the extreme, as illustrated by one of the restrictions that required that all the property of the colonists should be held in common for the first five years. The emigrants, however, were favored by one particular concession: that they should retain in the New World all the privileges and personal and social rights of Englishmen.

As early as August 1606, the Plymouth Company sent their first ship to America. This vessel, however, was captured by a Spanish man-of-war. Later in the year, another ship was dispatched by the company, spending the winter on the American coast.

The following summer a colony of 100 persons was sent to the mouth of the Kennebec River. A fort was built and named St. George. Things went well with the settlers for a while, but about half of the group returned to England. During the winter, the storehouse was burned and 60 people starved or froze to death. With the coming of summer, the survivors escaped to England.

The London Company met with greater success in their establishment of a colony in the region that Sir Walter Raleigh had named Virginia two decades before, when he established a settlement that was wiped out in 1588.

A group of three vessels was fitted out under the command of Christopher Newport, and in December 1606, the ships set sail for the New World. After a stop in the Canary Islands, the vessels reached the American coast in April of the following year. The leaders of the colony steered the fleet for Virginia's Roanoke Island, site of Raleigh's ill-fated colony, but a storm prevailed and the ships were borne northward into Chesapeake Bay.

On the southern shore, they found the mouth of a beautiful river that was

CAPTAIN BARTHOLOMEW GOSNOLD MAKES LANDFALL IN THE NEW WORLD.

THE CONFLICTING LONDON AND PLYMOUTH LAND GRANTS.

and enterprise of their remarkable leader, Captain John Smith. The other members of the corporation showed little in the way of management skills. Most were quite incompetent, and indeed some were also dishonest. Under John Smith's direction, however, Jamestown colony soon began to show signs of vitality and progress. The first settlers were afflicted with disease, but after Smith introduced various improvements in building and food supply, the health of the settlers was restored. Smith also explored and mapped the Chesapeake region, mapping that broad and important water and naming its tributaries. In exploring the area, Smith was taken prisoner by Native Americans, and Powhatan, the chief of the Native American confederacy in the region, condemned him to die.

According to legend, Smith's life was saved by Matoaka (known as Pocahontas), the daughter of Powhatan. She is said to have shielded Smith's head from the uplifted clubs with her own head. The decree of death was reversed, and Smith was permitted to live.

By the time Smith returned to Jamestown, Captain Newport had returned from England with a cargo of supplies and a new group of immigrants.

named in honor of King James. Proceeding up this stream about 50 miles, Newport chose a peninsula on the northern bank as the site of his Virginia settlement. The colonists debarked and the ships were moored by the shore.

Here, in May 1607, the foundations of Jamestown, the oldest successful English settlement in America, were laid. This was 110 years after the first landing on North America by John Cabot. Nearly 42 years had elapsed since the founding of St. Augustine. The London Company had beat its rival in establishing an American colony, and for several years the Plymouth Company made little progress.

At first, Jamestown was badly managed, but the fortune of the colonists was at length restored by the valor, industry

For two years, the colony was shaped by Smith's masterly hand. In 1609, however, while sleeping in a boat on the James River, he was wounded by the explosion of a bag of gunpowder. After enduring great suffering from his wound, he delegated his authority to Sir George Percy and sought medical and surgical aid in England.

In the autumn of 1609, Smith left the scene of his toils and sufferings, never to return. His loss was soon seriously felt in the colony. The coming winter, known as "the starving time," found the colonists pushed to the edge of desperation, and in the following spring it was decided that they would abandon Jamestown and return to England. However, just as the settlers sailed out of the mouth of the James River, the ships of Lord Delaware came into sight with additional emigrants and abundant supplies. The colonists quickly turned around and returned to their abandoned houses.

Lord Delaware took over the management of the Virginia government, and he was succeeded by Sir Thomas Dale, and he, in turn, by Sir Thomas Gates. The latter held office until 1614, when Dale was recalled. In 1617, Gates himself returned to England.

In 1617, Samuel Argall was chosen governor and began an administration noted for fraud and oppression rather than wise and humane policy. For two years he remained in authority, but the discontent of the colonists led to his recall and the appointment of Sir George Yeardley in his place.

It was during Yeardley's administration that a better form of civil management was introduced. The territory of the colony was divided into eleven districts, called boroughs, and the governor issued a proclamation that the citizens of each borough would select two representatives to constitute a legislative assembly. Elections were held, and in July 1619, the delegates convened at Jamestown as the Virginia House of Burgesses, or the Colonial Legislature, the first popular assembly held in the Western Hemisphere.

As an interesting footnote pertaining to the early development and expansion of the colony, it should be mentioned that in the early years, very few families emigrated to Virginia. Thus, in the fall of 1620, young women were invited to cast their fortunes and seek husbands among the Virginia colonists.

MATOAKA, KNOWN AS POCAHONTAS, LATER MARRIED JOHN ROLFE AND TOOK THE ENGLISH NAME REBECCA.

THE PLYMOUTH COLONY

The idea of a colony in America was proposed, and John Carver (1575-1621) and Robert Cushman were dispatched from Leyden to London to meet with agents of the London Company and the Plymouth Company. The businessmen gave them some encouragement, but King James I and his ministers were against all measures that might seem to favor a group they thought of as "heretics." The most that King James would do was to give the Puritans an informal promise that he would leave them alone in America.

The Puritans resolved to seek a new home in the wilds of America, with or without the king's permission. They scraped together the money to hire two ships, the *Speedwell* and the *Mayflower*, for their voyage across the Atlantic. The *Speedwell* was to carry the emigrants from Leyden to Southampton, where they were to be joined by the *Mayflower* with another group from London.

The Puritan congregation in Leyden followed the emigrants to the shore. There, under the open skies, their pastor, John Robinson, gave them a parting address and benediction. Both vessels set sail from England, but the *Speedwell* was found to be unfit for ocean sailing, so it returned to port.

The *Mayflower* had a stormy voyage of over two months, but early on November 9, the ship anchored in Cape Cod Bay. A meeting was held on board and a Compact, or agreement, was adopted for the government of the

THE ENGLISH SHIP MAYFLOWER.

THE PILGRIMS DRAFTED THE MAYFLOWER COMPACT ABOARD THEIR SHIP. IT WAS A STEP TOWARD CIVIL EQUALITY . . . BUT IT APPLIED ONLY TO MEN.

colony that would be established. The emigrants declared their loyalty to the English crown and agreed to live together in peace and harmony, with equal rights to all and obeying just laws made for the common good.

For several days the *Mayflower* lay at anchor while the boats were repaired and preparations made for debarkation. Captain Miles Standish led a small group ashore to explore the area and select a potential settlement site. Having found nothing suitable, they returned to the ship. With snow and sleet falling, the ship was steered around the coast until it was driven, half by accident and half by the skill of the pilot, into the safe haven on the west side of the bay. Here, on December 21, 1620, the people, remembered today as "the Pilgrims," landed on the shore of what is now Massachusetts. According to legend, their first footfall in the New World was on a boulder that was subsequently known as Plymouth Rock, after the name of the port city in England that would be the namesake for the Pilgrims' settlement.

The sleet and snow blew upon them in alternate tempests. The immigrants were sick, and would soon be dying of hunger, cold and despair. A few days were spent in explorations along the coast, but a site was chosen near the first landing. Trees were felled and the snowdrifts cleared away. In January 1621, they began to build New Plymouth. Each man was responsible for building his own house, but the ravages of disease grew worse daily. Strong arms fell powerless. At one time, only seven men were able to work on the construction of shelters. Starvation was avoided only by the doling out of a few kernels of corn. If an early spring had not come with sunshine, bird song and gladness, the colony would have perished.

Although Governor John Carver, his family, and half of the colony died, the rest went forward with courageous spirits. Those who survived rose from the snows of winter to plant and build and sing their hymns of thankfulness.

Miles Standish went out with six soldiers to gather information about the surrounding area, but they failed in their attempts to make contact with the Native Americans.

Soon after, however, Samoset, a leader of the Wampanoag tribe, came into Plymouth, offered his hand, and welcomed the strangers. He could speak some English, for he'd been with the Europeans at intervals since the time of the earlier voyages. He told them of his people and of a great plague that had killed many people a few years earlier. A short time later, another Native American named Squanto, who had been to England and learned to speak English, visited Plymouth and confirmed what Samoset had said.

Later in the spring, the colonists were introduced to Massasoit, the great chief of the Wampanoags, and with him they entered into a treaty that remained inviolate for 50 years.

The agreement was simple, providing that no injury should be done by the Europeans to Native Americans or by Native Americans to them, and that all offenders should be given up by either party for punishment according to the laws of the two peoples. Later, nine of the other leading tribes entered into similar relations with the English.

Though there would continue to be difficult times for the Plymouth colony, their third year, 1623, brought a plentiful harvest, and the people of Plymouth began to share their agricultural products with the Native Americans, who brought wild game to exchange for corn. This season of abundance and sharing is commemorated today in our holiday of Thanksgiving, although the holiday itself was not set aside until the twentieth century.

Meanwhile, the main body of Puritans remained in Leyden. John Robinson, their leader, made strenuous efforts to bring his people to America, but the London adventurers who managed the earlier enterprise refused to furnish money or transportation, and at the end

SAMOSET GREETING THE COLONISTS IN PLYMOUTH.

of the fourth year there were fewer than 200 Europeans in New England.

In spite of this, Cape Ann was settled in 1624 by a group of Puritans from Dorchester, England, that were led by their minister, John White. The place chosen for the colony, however, was found to be unfavorable, and after two years the whole group moved southward to found the settlement that would evolve into the city of Salem.

Two years later, a second group arrived with John Endicott, who was chosen governor. The colonists obtained a patent from Charles I, and the settlements were incorporated under the name of the governor and the Company of Massachusetts Bay in New England.

Also in 1626, another 200 immigrants arrived, some of whom settled at Plymouth, while the rest moved to the peninsula on the north side of Boston harbor and laid the foundations of Charlestown. In 1630, about 300 of the best Puritan families in England came to America under the direction of John Winthrop, who was chosen governor. Though a royalist by birth, he cast in his lot with those favoring a republic.

Although he was an an Episcopalian himself, he chose to suffer affliction with the Puritans. Surrounded with affluence and comfort at home, he left this to share the uncertain destiny of a new life with the Pilgrims in America.

After Plymouth, the settlements on the Merrimac River were the oldest in New England. In 1622, the area between the Merrimac and Kennebec rivers, reaching from the Atlantic to the St. Lawrence, was granted by the Council of Plymouth to Sir Ferdinand Gorges and John Mason. In the spring of 1623, two small groups of emigrants were sent out by Mason and Gorges to survey the area, which had been explored as early as 1614 by John Smith. The progress of the colony, however, was slow and the first villages were no more than fishing stations. After six years, the proprietors divided their dominion between them, Gorges taking the northern part and Mason receiving the southern portion of the province. John Wheelwright purchased the rights to the territory occupied by Mason's colony. A second patent was issued to the proprietary, and the name of the province was changed from Laconia to New Hampshire.

CHIEF MASSASOIT CONFIRMS A PEACE TREATY AT PLYMOUTH.

THE EARLY FRENCH COLONIES

The French obtained a footing in Nova Scotia and on the banks of the St. Lawrence. The English colonized the country around Massachusetts Bay. The Dutch established themselves on Manhattan Island and in detached settlements along the Hudson and Delaware rivers. Inland from Chesapeake Bay, Jamestown was well established, removing all doubts of its permanency. In Florida, the Spaniards succeeded in establishing St. Augustine and several other successful settlements. Far to the west, in the heart of the continent, Santa Fe was the northern outpost of Spanish influence.

Beyond the lure of adventure and the wonder of new sights in a new land that was shared by all, each of the European powers viewed the economic development of North America in a different way.

The English came primarily to establish a permanent presence on the land itself. The Dutch came as traders. The Spanish came for gold. The French also came for gold, but discovered wealth in furs.

While the Spanish searched the Southwest for gold mines, the French explored the St. Lawrence River and the Great Lakes country. Beaver were plentiful and the French discovered that their fur was of a high quality. During the seventeenth century, while maintaining a steady stream of beaver pelts to Europe, French trappers and traders reached deeper into the heart of what is now the United States than any other nationality.

In 1623, Etienne Brule became the first European to see Lake Superior, not only the largest of the Great Lakes, but also the largest body of fresh water on Earth.

With the trappers and traders came the priests, who saw their goal as bringing the message of Christianity to the Native Americans. By mid-century, French trading posts and missions could be found in what are now Michigan, Ontario and Wisconsin. In 1673, in the most comprehensive expedition to date, Father Jacques Marquette (1637-1675) and Louis Joliet (1645-1700) traveled from the headwaters of the Fox River to the headwaters of the Mississippi River and then down the Mississippi. They traveled south as far as the Arkansas

River, reached by Hernando DeSoto (1496-1542) 133 years before. Marquette and Joliet then turned north and became the first Europeans to camp on the site of what is now Chicago.

Although the French made a general claim of sovereignty over the lands of the interior, aside from establishing small forts and posts, they did little to disturb the Native American possession of them. The most important of these French settlements were Detroit, Michilimackinac, Kaskaskia, Cahokia and Vincennes. The fur trade with the Indians dominated the economy and much of the daily activity.

The first man to lead an expedition tracing the entire route of the mighty Mississippi from headwaters to mouth was the great French explorer Rene Robert Cavalier Sieur de LaSalle (1643-1687). Having built a ship above Niagara Falls, the LaSalle expedition sailed through Lake Erie, Lake Huron and Lake Michigan. When the ship was damaged, LaSalle and part of his team hiked

1,000 miles back to Fort Frontenac, while Father Louis Hennepin (1640-1701) continued on to the Mississippi River and reached the present site of Minneapolis and St. Paul.

In 1681, LaSalle reached the Mississippi himself and canoed all the way to the Gulf of Mexico. In 1682, he founded Louisiana (named for King Louis XIV) before returning to Quebec. Traveling to France, he convinced Louis XIV to take an interest in the development of his namesake colony, a vast region of 828,000 square miles that included the Mississippi and all its tributaries. Today's state of Louisiana, by contrast, contains only 52,457 square miles of the lower part of old French Louisiana.

In 1684, the king authorized four ships and 280 people for LaSalle's Louisiana effort and an expedition sailed for the mouth of the Mississippi. Blown off course, they made landfall in Texas instead, and LaSalle decided to lead a party overland to the Mississippi. Instead, he traveled far enough to the west to reach the Colorado River. En route back to the east, LaSalle was shot and killed by two of his own men before the group finally reached the Mississippi.

France did not abandon the vast area of Louisiana, and French trappers and traders became the primary European influence throughout the Mississippi drainage as well as the Great Lakes country. Founded in 1718 by Jean Baptiste le Moyne, Ville d'Orleans (now New Orleans) became a major metropolis. Major trading centers were also established up river at Baton Rouge, Natchez and St. Louis.

MARQUETTE AND JOLIET ON THE MISSISSIPPI.

17

THE DEVELOPMENT OF NEW ENGLAND

After Plymouth, another very important English colony was the Massachusetts Bay Colony, established north of Plymouth in 1628 under John Endicott. He brought his family and about 100 others to settle on a spot then called Naumkeag, now known as Salem. Like those of the parent colony, the settlers were Puritans who desired greater liberty in matters of religious worship and doctrine. Associated with Endicott were John Winthrop, Isaac Johnson, Matthew Cradock, Thomas Goff and Sir Richard Saltonstall.

In 1629, the Massachusetts Company was confirmed by King Charles I, who granted it the powers of civil government, and the seat of the colony's government was transferred from London to Massachusetts Bay. At the same time, a new election of officers of the colony took place. John Winthrop was chosen governor, and Thomas Dudley deputy governor. Soon after their appointment, they sailed with a large group, some of whom settled at Mishawam and Charlestown, while others went to Boston, as well as to Watertown, Dorchester, Roxbury and Lynn. The first General Court of the colony was held at Boston in October 1630. In the following years, the people of the Massachusetts colony extended their settlements as far away as Connecticut and Rhode Island.

The area that is now Rhode Island was settled by Roger Williams, a Salem clergyman who had ironically been ban-

GOVERNOR JOHN WINTHROP

ished due to his religious views, even though they embodied the true principles of religious liberty on which the parent colony was founded.

The principles of religious belief as well as social and political organization which Williams adopted were among the most liberal and tolerant of those which had been proclaimed since the beginning of the Reformation. He assumed that the conscience of the individual could not be bound by the magistrate or the civil government, and furthermore, that the government's power extended only to the collection of taxes, the restraint of law breakers, the punishment of crime, and the protection of all in the enjoyment of equal rights.

It was for these ideas that he was expelled from Plymouth colony, driven away in the dead of winter and obliged to live off the land for over three months in the snow, sleeping in hollow trees and subsisting on parched corn, acorns and roots.

He went among the Native Americans whose rights he had defended and was entertained by Massasoit of the Wampanoags and Canonicum of the Naragansetts. In 1636, he and his followers put down roots in a place they named Providence.

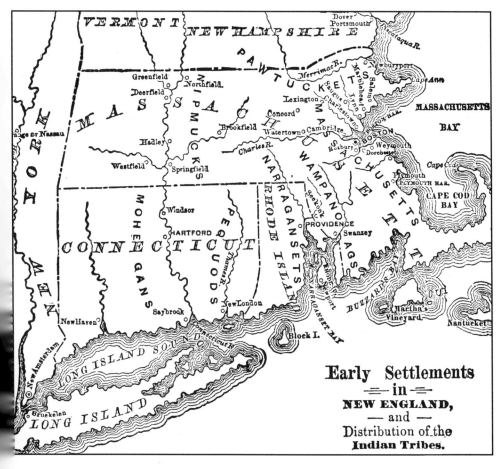

Early Settlements
— in —
NEW ENGLAND,
— and —
Distribution of the
Indian Tribes.

No man of the period, nor possibly in the history of New England, deserves more enduring fame, not so much for what he did in the founding of a successful colony, but for his relations with Native Americans. He won their friendship, thus saving the colonists several times from massacre. The Narragansetts and Pequods were hereditary enemies, but through the persuasion of Williams, they became reconciled and made a treaty of friendship with the English.

The detente was short-lived, however, for the Pequods both feared and distrusted the English. They formed an alliance with the Narragansetts and Mohegans, whom they persuaded to join them in a war. When the situation became critical, Williams notified Sir Henry Vane, the governor of Massachusetts, of the peril.

He then went alone to the Narragansett camp. For two days he pleaded with leaders to stand by their vows of peace. He convinced the Naragansetts, and without their allies, the Pequods were easily defeated by the English militia.

The Puritans brought a religious toleration for themselves to America, but were not as forthcoming in their toleration for others. They had inherited the vice of narrow-mindedness from the Middle Ages. As a consequence, religious dissension appeared in the colony, and it was this condition that led to Roger Williams' expulsion from Salem.

Another important dissident was Anne Hutchinson, a brilliant and foresighted leader, who came over in the ship with Sir Henry Vane. She claimed the privilege of speaking at the weekly meetings. This was refused by the elders because "Women have no business at these assemblies, and most of them need their tongues bridled at times like common scolds."

Anne Hutchinson denounced the ministers for defrauding women of the benefits of the gospels, and was, in turn, declared to be unfit for the society of Christians. With a large number of friends, she was banished from Massachusetts. In 1638, this new group of exiles, led by John Clarke, William Coddington and Anne Hutchinson, arrived at Rhode Island. The exiles left Massachusetts intending to found a new colony on the Delaware River, but Roger Williams welcomed them, and Sir Henry Vane, still the governor of Massachusetts, convinced the native Narragansett people to give the exiles the island of Rhode Island, and so it was here that the colony was established in March 1641. Portsmouth was founded and the little band concluded that they would take ancient Israel as a model to frame their social structure. They accordingly established a little theocracy, and William Coddington was elected judge.

One of the earliest colonies in New England after Plymouth was Connecticut. It began in 1630 as a grant to the Earl of Warwick under the auspices of the Council of Plymouth, the successor to the Plymouth Company. However, there were already conflicting claims on the region. Dutch settlers from Manhattan had built an outpost on the Connecticut River and New Plymouth's colonists carried their territorial claim westward indefinitely, extending beyond the Connecticut and the Hudson rivers and including the Dutch settlements of New Netherland.

In 1635, John Winthrop, Jr. arrived in New England bearing a mandate from the "proprietaries" of the western colony — Lord Say and Lord Brooke — to fortify the mouth of the Connecticut River and to expel the Dutch from that region. These noblemen, in accordance with their grant, had chosen the country of the Connecticut as the scene of their colony.

The fort that was built at the entrance to the river was called Saybrook, so named in honor of the proprietors. Thus the colony of Connecticut was established, and this in turn would further the spread of more settlements in New England.

Some of the colonists arriving in what is now Massachusetts settled at Salem. Others paused at Charlestown and Watertown, and others founded Roxbury and Dorchester. The governor

ROGER WILLIAMS CONFERRING WITH NATIVE AMERICANS NEAR PROVIDENCE.

himself, with a few other families, crossed the harbor to the peninsula called Shawmut. Here they laid the foundation of Boston, destined to be the capital of the colony and the metropolis of New England. As in Virginia, people in Massachusetts tended from the first toward the ideals of democratic government.

As early as 1634, the Puritan colonists established a representative form of government in spite of the strenuous opposition of several ministers, notably the sharp-tongued Cotton Mather. On election day, the assembly listened attentively and then went on to approve a democratic system. A ballot box was substituted for the old method of public voting. The restriction on the right of suffrage, by which only church members were permitted to vote, was also overturned.

The Puritans abroad had come to see that it was worthwhile to live in a country where the principles of freedom were spreading with such rapidity, and in 1634, about 3,000 new colonists arrived under the leadership of Hugh Peters and Sir Henry Vane.

However, these new immigrants found the settlements around Massachusetts Bay overcrowded. It seemed that there would not be room for the incoming immigrants from Europe, so the more adventurous soon began to plunge into the wilderness to find new places to settle. One small group of twelve families, under the leadership of Simon Willard and Peter Bulkeley, marched through the woods until they reached some open meadowlands only 16 miles west of Boston. Here the foundation of

Concord was laid. Later in the same year, another branch colony of 60 persons made their way westward to the Connecticut River, and in the following spring, they founded Windsor and Hartford.

While intolerance darkened the Puritan character, many virtues illumined it. It was what an artist might call a chiaroscuro, meaning that, on the whole, the light shone through the darkness. While the Puritans stooped to being persecutors for opinion's sake, in many cases they rose to the level of philanthropists. In 1636, the colony appropriated money to found and endow a college. The measure met with popular favor, and the project went forward to success. Newtown was selected as the sight for the proposed school. Plymouth, Salem and the villages in the Connecticut valley sent contributions. In 1638, on his deathbed, John Harvard, a minister in Charlestown, bequeathed his library and a small fortune to the institution. To perpetuate the memory of this benefactor, the new school was named Harvard College, and to honor the college in England where many of the leading men of Massachusetts had been educated, the name of Newtown was changed to Cambridge.

In 1638, Stephen Daye, an English printer, arrived in Boston and set up his press at Cambridge. His first publication was a New England almanac published for 1639. Thomas Welde and John Eliot, two ministers from Roxbury, translated the Hebrew Psalms into English verse, and published their work in a 300-page volume that was the first book printed on the west side of the Atlantic.

By 1640, one could count 300 ships at anchor in Massachusetts Bay, but not all had been constructed in Europe. William Stephens, a shipbuilder who came with the immigrants of 1629, built and launched a 400-ton American vessel.

By this time the population of the Massachusetts Bay area surpassed 20,000. As the colonies grew, the question of uniting them under one civil government had come up in the assemblies of Massachusetts and its neighboring colonies. They joined in a loose confederacy called the United Colonies of New England. The chief authority was vested in a General Assembly, which was composed of two representatives who were chosen annually from each colony. Since the colonies were under the general authority of the English King, no President other than the Speaker of the Assembly was specified.

The sentiments of the people of Massachusetts with respect to the English Revolution of 1642 were very different from those of the people of Virginia, who were in sympathy with the king. The friends of the Puritans had made their way into the English House of Commons, where they supported Oliver Cromwell. Throughout the English Civil War, the American Puritans supported the Revolutionary party. Distance, however, modified the feelings of the people of New England, and when Charles I was brought to the block, those whose parents had been exiled by his father lamented his tragic fate and preserved the memory of his virtues.

Cromwell understood perfectly the temper and sentiments of the American colonists. He remained from first to last their steadfast friend. When the era of the English commonwealth drew to a close and Charles II was restored to the throne, Edward Whalley and William Goffe, two of the judges who had passed the sentence of death on Charles I, escaped to Massachusetts. Governor John Endicott received them with courtesy, but the agents of the British Government followed in hot pursuit. The people of Boston helped the judges to escape to New Haven. No one, not even the Native Americans, accepted the reward that was offered for the judges' apprehension, and they safely reached the village of Hadley, in the valley of the Connecticut River, where they remained for the rest of their lives.

In 1644, the outbreak of war between England and the Netherlands furnished an opportunity to Charles II to recover the American colonies from their proprietary, chartered and semi-independent status. It became necessary at the beginning of the war to send a British fleet to America in order to capture the Dutch colonies on the Hudson, and the king used the same strike force to intimidate the English-speaking colonies that owed their political existence to charters and guarantees given by former kings.

Charles II also sent four royal commissioners to America to sit in judgment of disputes and intercolonial controversy. He believed that the colonists' acceptance of a court of arbitration would lead to a recognition of the royal authority in political matters. The commissioners arrived in July 1664, but the Americans gave the royal judges a cold reception.

WILLIAM PENN IN PENNSYLVANIA

In England, the Society of Friends, known as "the Quakers," were a persecuted religious minority subject to imprisonment and exile. It was under these conditions that Society leader William Penn and his associates conceived the project of establishing a complete and glorious refuge for the afflicted Quakers in the unoccupied wilds of America. Encouraged by the success of the flourishing settlement of New Jersey, Penn wanted to establish a free state founded on the optimistic principle of universal brotherhood on the banks of the Delaware River.

Penn went boldly to King Charles II and made his petition. In May 1681, he received a charter bearing the great seal of England and the signature of the king. The grant was complicated. Penn held a sizable claim due to his father's estate against the British government. He agreed to relinquish this in exchange for the grant and charter. Penn was made the proprietary of the territory bounded east by the Delaware, extending north and south through three degrees of latitude, and westward through five degrees of longitude. The area would be called Pennsylvania, meaning simply, "Penn's Woodlands." Only the three counties comprising the present state of Delaware were reserved for the Duke of York.

William Penn was the son of a vice admiral who, early in his life, converted to the Christian faith. William eventually embraced the tenets of the Society of Friends. His father was both grieved and

QUAKER LEADER WILLIAM PENN

displeased, and spared no efforts to induce him to renounce those peculiarities of manners and practice that William's religious views impelled him to adopt.

But neither his attending the university, nor his foreign travel, nor occasional time spent away from the confines of his parent's home, changed William's eccentricities.

In Pennsylvania, Penn openly declared his purpose to found a free commonwealth without respect to the color, race or religion of its inhabitants. He believed that the friendship of Native Americans might be earned by a policy of justice and humanity, that a refuge might be established for all peoples who might choose for conscience's sake to flee the oppression and hardships of their European homes.

In an incredibly short time, three shiploads of Quaker emigrants were sent from England to the land of promise. With these came William Markham, agent of the proprietary and deputy governor of the new province.

Penn exerted himself in a quest for peace with all. He wrote to the Swedish settlers who had established themselves in the area covered by his charter, and told them that they would be in no way disturbed.

He also instructed his deputy to seek friendship with the Native Americans. He sent a letter directly to the native chiefs, assuring them of his honest purposes and brotherly intentions.

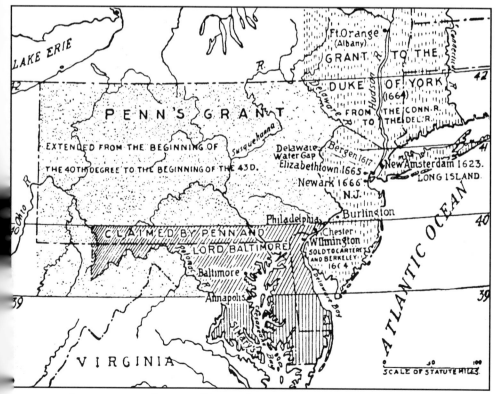

A OVERVIEW OF ENGLISH MIDDLE ATLANTIC LAND GRANTS, CIRCA 1666.

PHILADELPHIA AND VICINITY

Penn next drew up a frame of government that conceded everything to the people, even allowing them to accept or reject the constitution that he drafted to govern the settlement. The world had never witnessed a powerful governor with such confidence in the righteousness of human nature and the essential integrity of man. With extraordinary skill and confidence, Penn approached the Duke of York and induced him to surrender the three counties in Delaware to the Quaker colony.

In the summer of 1682, Penn made his own preparations to depart for America and wrote a letter of farewell to the Friends in England. A large group of emigrants sailed with him to Newcastle near the mouth of the Delaware River, where they were met not only by the Quaker immigrants, but by Swedes, Dutch and English who came to greet the new governor.

He made a speech on the day of his arrival, renewing his former pledges and exhorting the people to sobriety and honesty. He then sailed upriver as far as Chester. He passed the site of Philadelphia and visited the settlements of the Friends in western New Jersey. He crossed the province to New York and Long Island, speaking to the Quakers in Brooklyn.

Meanwhile, Markham, the deputy governor, had established good relations with the Native Americans of the neighboring tribes, so after the return of Penn from New York, a great conference was held with the native chiefs. The council was held under the open sky. Clad in the plain garb of the Quakers and accompanied by a few unarmed Friends, Penn came to the appointed spot and took his place under a venerable elm. The chiefs sat in a semicircle. Speaking with quiet demeanor through his interpreter, Penn said:

"My Friends, we have met on the broad pathway of good faith. We are all on flesh and blood. Being brethren, no advantage shall be taken on either side. When disputes arise we will settle them in council. Between us there shall be nothing but openness and love."

The chiefs replied, "While the rivers run and the sun shines we will live in peace with the children of William Penn."

This simple compact was not put in writing, but it was long observed with fidelity by both peoples. No deed of violence or injustice on the part of either is recorded for the roughly 70 years that the province remained under the control of the Friends.

The rapid growth of the Pennsylvania colony made a legislative assembly necessary to the general welfare, and in December 1682, a general convention of the colonists was held at Chester. The work of the body occupied three days, and at the close of the session, Penn delivered an address and left to visit Lord Baltimore, with whom he had an important conference concerning the boundaries between the two provinces.

At the same time, Penn was looking for a site for a new city to serve as the centerpiece of the type of colony that he hoped Pennsylvania could be. The neck of land between the Schuylkill River and the Delaware River was chosen and purchased from the Swedes.

The forest still covered these lands, and the chestnut, walnut and ash trees furnished the names for the city's streets. By 1683, Penn was laying out the streets for Philadelphia, "the City of Brotherly Love." The plan for Penn's new capital contained houses and was soon home to over 2,000 people.

Schools were established and the printing press began its work. In another year, Philadelphia had outgrown New York. The city grew in the same spirit with which it had been founded, with a sense of security and cooperation among neighbors.

A KITCHEN IN A TYPICAL EIGHTEENTH CENTURY COLONIAL HOME.

MARYLAND, THE CAROLINAS AND GEORGIA

The religious struggle that had prevailed for over a century, since the beginning of the Reformation, clearly played a role in shaping the face of the New World, from Plymouth to the French Huguenot colonies on the St. Lawrence River. Such was the case with a new colony north of Virginia that was established by Sir George Calvert (1580-1632) of Yorkshire. Educated at Oxford, he had devoted much of his life to travel and study. An ardent Catholic, he was a member of the Anglo-Irish peerage with the title Lord Baltimore.

In Protestant England, however, the Catholics were in disfavor, and the dominant Church of England persecuted both the Catholics and the dissenting Protestants. With this in mind, Calvert obtained a patent from King James I in 1623 for a colony in southern Newfoundland. However, it was a desolate place where only fishing was possible and where the French harassed English fishing boats.

Against this backdrop, Lord Baltimore decided to turn his attention to the appealing countryside surrounding Chesapeake Bay. In 1629, he visited Virginia and was favorably received by the Assembly. That body offered him citizenship, but only if he would renounce Catholicism. He pleaded for toleration, but the Assembly would not yield and Calvert was obliged to turn away.

In the meantime, the London Company had dissolved and the King of England recovered the rights and privileges he had formerly conceded to that corpo-

SIR GEORGE CALVERT (LORD BALTIMORE)

28

ration. It was therefore within his power to re-grant the vast territory north of the Potomac River, which by the terms of the second charter had earlier been conceded to Virginia. When the Assembly refused toleration to Baltimore, he appealed to the king for a charter for himself and his colony. King Charles I accepted the proposal, and the charter was drawn and received the royal signature. By their intolerance, the Virginians saved their religion and lost a province.

The territory granted to Sir George Calvert was ample. It extended, according to the phraseology of the times, "from ocean to ocean." The boundary on the north was the 40th parallel. On the west the limit was a line drawn due south from the 40th parallel to the westernmost extent of the Potomac, which would constitute the southern boundary. In honor of Henrietta Maria, the daughter of Henry IV of France and the wife of King Charles, the name of Maryland was conferred on the new province. A glance at the map will show that the original grant included the present states of Maryland and Delaware, as well as a large part of Pennsylvania and New Jersey.

On the whole, the charter issued to Sir George was the most liberal that an English king had yet granted. Christianity was declared to be the state religion, but no preference was given to sect or creed. The lives and property of the colonists were put under the careful protection of English law. Free trade was declared as the policy of the province, and arbitrary taxation was forbidden. The appointment of officers in the colonial government was conceded to Sir George, but the right of making and amending the laws would be in the hands of a popular assembly.

In 1632, before the colony was fully established, Sir George died, and his son Cecil (or Cecilius) Calvert (1605-1675) took over the task of establishing a free state in the New World. In 1633, a group of 200 was collected for the voyage. However, Cecil, the new Lord Baltimore, changed his mind about going to America himself and appointed his brother, Leonard Calvert (1606-1647), to act as governor. In March 1634, the Catholic immigrants arrived at Old Point Comfort with a letter from the king requesting that Governor Harvey of Virginia receive the newcomers with courtesy. The governor was obliged to obey, but the Virginians were jealous and upset about the possibility of losing the profitable fur trade on the upper Chesapeake.

Sailing north into the bay, Leonard Calvert and his colony entered the Potomac. After some exploration, they selected the country at the mouth of the St. Mary's for their settlement. Here the colonists took possession of a half-abandoned Native American town, purchased the surrounding territory, set up a cross as the sign of Catholic occupation, and gave the name of St. Mary's to this, the oldest colony of Maryland.

By the middle of the seventeenth century, the area south of Virginia, which had been known to the French as Carolina after their King Charles IX, was beginning to attract a good deal of interest from the various English-speaking colonies. In 1642, a group of Virginia adventurers obtained permission from the Assembly to open trade with the Native Americans south of Roanoke Island. In 1651, they established a settlement at the mouth of the Chowan River. Soon after, William Clayborne of Maryland explored this part of the coast, and in 1661, a group of New England Puritans entered the Cape Fear River. They purchased land from the Native Americans and established a colony on Oldtown Creek, nearly 200 miles further south than any other English settlement.

Meanwhile, the settlement at the mouth of the river Chowan flourished. William Drummond was chosen governor in 1663, and the settlement was named the Albemarle County Colony.

Also in 1663, Edward Hyde (Lord Clarendon, 1609-1674), General George Monck (the Duke of Albemarle 1608-1670) and six other noblemen received a patent from the English King Charles II for all the country between the 36th parallel and the St. Johns River in Florida. However, in 1638, it was discovered that the Albemarle settlement was north of the 36th parallel and therefore beyond the limits of the grant to Clarendon and Monck. To remedy this, the northern boundary of Carolina was fixed at 36 degrees and 30 minutes, a line that has remained the southern limits of Virginia.

The Puritan settlement on Cape Fear River was broken up by hostile Native Americans, but soon after, the region, including the settlement site, was purchased by planters from Barbados. They laid out a new territory called Clarendon County and appointed Sir John Yeamans as governor. Clarendon prospered, but it was not until 1670 that English settlers made their way into what is now South Carolina.

At that time, there were no European settlements between the Cape Fear and the St. Johns rivers, even though the area was among the most attractive on the whole American coast.

The leaders of this venture, Joseph West and William Sayle, came by way of Barbados, steered far to the mouth, and reached the mainland near the Savannah River's mouth. The vessels entered the harbor of Port Royal 108 years after John Ribault, the leader of the Huguenots, had erected on the island a rude stone memorial bearing the lilies and emblems of France. But France had failed to colonize the area, and the Englishmen considered it fair game.

As in the case of Pennsylvania, the colony of Georgia was the product of a benevolent impulse. Struck with compassion at the miserable condition of the English poor, the English philanthropist James Oglethorpe conceived the idea of forming a colony for them in America. The chief abuse that the poor of England were subjected to was imprisonment for debt. Thousands of laborers had become indebted to the rich and were then arrest-

GEORGIA FOUNDER JAMES OGLETHORPE

ed and thrown into jail, leaving their families to face misery and starvation.

In 1728, Oglethorpe was appointed by Parliament at his own request to look into the conditions of the English poor and report measures of relief. Oglethorpe was a loyalist and an Oxford man by education. He was a churchman, a cavalier, a soldier and a member of Parliament. In his personal character, he was benevolent, generous, sympathetic and brave. He proposed that the victims of poverty should be set free from the debtor jails and be able to return to their families. However, the liberated prisoners were faced with further debt and were disheartened and disgraced. Oglethorpe appealed to King George II for the privilege of granting a colony in America, and on June 9, 1732, a royal charter was issued. Territory on the Savannah River was granted to a corporation to be held in trust for the poor for 21 years. In honor of the king, the new province was called Georgia.

During the summer and autumn Oglethorpe collected a colony of 120 persons. The emigrant ships left England in November and reached Charleston in January of 1733. After some exploration, the high bluff on which the city of Savannah now stands was selected as the settlement's site. Here, in February, they laid out the broad streets and public square of the oldest English town south of the Savannah River.

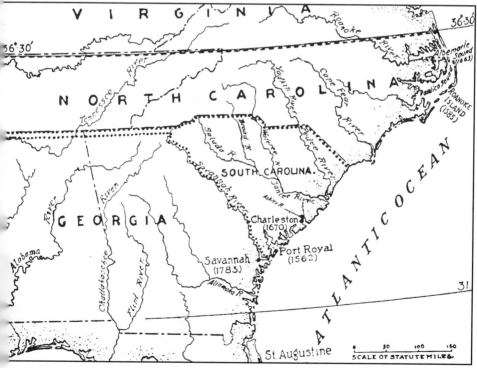

AN OVERVIEW OF THE SOUTHERN COLONIES AFTER THE PARTITION OF CAROLINA IN 1663.

VIRGINIA DEVELOPS

At the time of the outbreak of the English Civil War in 1640, Virginia sympathized with the king rather than the Parliamentarians. In the first year of the bloody struggle against the king, Sir William Berkeley came out to Virginia as royal governor and, with the exception of a brief visit to England in 1645, he remained in office for 10 years. Berkeley was a man of great administrative abilities, and notwithstanding the political disturbance in the Old World, Virginia prospered. The colonial laws were improved in many particulars and were made more compatible with the laws of England. The long existing controversies about the Virginia land titles were amicably settled. Cruel punishments were abolished, and the taxes equalized.

Nevertheless, Berkeley was a thorough loyalist, and to this extent there was discord between him and those colonists who favored democracy. Most of the Virginians, however, adhered to the cause of Charles I, even to the day of his death in 1649. When the monarch was beheaded and a commonwealth declared, they proclaimed his son Charles II to be the rightful ruler of both England and the American colonies.

Oliver Cromwell, the Lord High Protector of the Commonwealth and the new ruler of England, was naturally offended at this conduct by the Virginians. He was determined to use force against them to bring about submission and ordered a warship sent into

ENGLAND'S KING CHARLES II

Chesapeake Bay. However, at the last minute, he decided to also send commissioners of the commonwealth to make overtures of peace to the colonists. They were told to carry an olive branch in one hand and a sword in the other.

By this time, it became apparent that the cause of England's Stuart kings was — for the time being — hopeless. Perceiving that their loyalty to an overthrown House was out of season the people of Virginia began negotiating with Cromwell's delegates. They wisely acknowledged the supreme authority of Parliament, and Cromwell was thus not obliged to employ force against his subjects.

Nevertheless, the English commonwealth failed, and in 1660, Charles II was restored to his ancestors' throne. He came to his ancient regal birthright as one might acquire the inheritance of an estate. He chose to consider the British Empire personal property to be used for the benefit of himself and his courtiers. In order to reward the profligates and hangers-on who thronged his court, he began to grant to them large tracts of land in Virginia. Suddenly, the men and women who redeemed these lands from wilderness and cultivated them for a quarter of a century found their farms given away to a flatterer of the royal household. Finally, in 1673, Charles II gave away the whole state of Virginia! Lord Culpepper and the Earl of Arlington, two ignoble noblemen, received under the great seal a deed that granted them "all the dominion of land and water called Virginia" for 31 years.

Meanwhile, in the colony, Governor Berkeley's first administration had ended, but after the restoration of Charles II, he was recommissioned and stayed in office until 1676. The Virginians directed their discontent at Berkeley and rose in rebellion. This revolt was both coupled with and excused by a Native American war that occurred when the Susquehanna people became hostile. The refusal of the governor to support the people in the war with the Native Americans and to recognize young Nathaniel Bacon as their leader led to a rebellion. Lord Berkeley was expelled from Jamestown and driven across the Chesapeake. However, Bacon fell sick and died, the spirit of the insurrection failed, and the militia was easily dispersed. The governor then fully avenged himself for the wrongs that he had suffered, and the leaders of the revolt were seized and hanged.

At the close of Berkeley's administration, Lord Culpepper was appointed as governor for life. He arrived in 1680 and took up the duties of his office. His official conduct was marked with avarice and dishonesty. He was removed from office in 1684. Virginia went from being a proprietary government to a Royal province. Lord Howard of Effingham was appointed governor, and he, in turn, was succeeded by Francis Nicholson.

The administration of the latter was signalized by Reverend James Blair's founding of the College of William and Mary in Williamsburg in 1693. Named in honor of the new king and queen of England, it was, next to Harvard University (1636) in Massachusetts, the first institution of higher learning established in America. Thomas Jefferson, America's third president and author of the Declaration of Independence, and President James Monroe were both alumni of the college.

NEW NETHERLAND

In 1609, Henry Hudson, an English sea captain sailing for the Netherlands West India Company in Amsterdam, first set foot on Manhattan Island and sailed up the river that now bears his name. He claimed the region on behalf of his employer and returned to Europe after probing the New England coastline to the north.

As early as 1618, there was a trading post at Bergen, west of the Hudson, but 40 years passed before a permanent settlement was made here. In 1623, Fort Nassau was built by Cornelius May at the place where Timber Creek falls into the Delaware. However, he abandoned the outpost and returned to New Amsterdam. In 1629, the southern part of New Jersey was granted to two Dutch patrons named Godyn and Bloinaert, but the proprietaries made no attempt at settlement.

For ten years after the establishment of the first settlement on Manhattan, New Amsterdam was governed by directors appointed by the Dutch West India Company. In 1623, a new colony of 30 families headed by Cornelius May arrived at Manhattan. The immigrants, called Walloons, were Dutch Protestant refugees from Flanders. As such, they shared similar religious interests with the Huguenots of France and the Puritans of England, and like the others, the Walloons came to America to escape the persecutions that they were subjected to in their own country.

Cornelius May also sailed down the coast of New Jersey and entered and explored Delaware Bay. On his return in the following year, he was made first governor of New Netherland, an office whose duties were essentially that of the superintendent of a trading post. In 1625 he was succeeded in office by Willem Verhulst, and in 1626 Peter Minuit of Wesel was appointed by the Dutch West India Company as governor of New Netherland.

The population grew and the colony increased in strength and influence. In 1629, they prepared what was called Charter of Privileges, under which a class of proprietors was authorized to possess and colonize the surrounding countryside. Each patron might select for himself anywhere in New Netherland a tract of land "not more than 16 miles in length and of a breadth to be determined by the location." In accordance with the provisions of the charter, five states were soon established. Three of them were contiguous and located in the valley of the Hudson River above and below Fort Orange. The fourth was laid out by Michael de Pauw on Staten Island, and the fifth included the southern half of the present state of Delaware.

Perhaps the most historically important of the early governors of New Netherland was the soldierly Peter Stuyvesant (1592-1672), whose name is still remembered in the form of place names in and around New York City. He came out under commission of the Dutch West India Company in 1647. His influence over the colonists of Manhattan and the Hudson River valley was salutary, and the Dutch state began to improve under his administration. However, progress was slow. As late as the middle of the century, the better parts of Manhattan Island were still not yet cultivated, though divided among the Dutch farmers. What is now Central Park was still a forest of oak and chestnut trees.

In 1651, Augustine Herman purchased a considerable tract of land in what is now New Jersey, including the site of Elizabethtown. Seven years later the grant was enlarged so as to take in the trading post of Bergen. In 1663, a group of Puritans about to emigrate from Long Island obtained permission of Governor Stuyvesant to occupy the lands on the Raritan, but before their project could be carried out, the Dutch Government of New Amsterdam was overthrown by the English, and the English crown never recognized the land claims of the Dutch.

In the first quarter of the seventeenth century, Spain, France, England and the Netherlands succeeded in establishing permanent colonies. Sweden was the fifth, and the great King Gustavus Adolphus (1594-1632) was the patron of the enterprise. It was in 1626 that a group of Swedish merchants was organized to promote the emigration of a colony. Before this could be carried out, Gustavus Adolphus was killed in battle in 1632, and the work was transmitted to the Swedish minister Count Axel Gustafsson Oxenstjerna (1583-1654). The charter that the late king had given to the company was renewed, and after four years of preparation, the enterprise was brought to a successful issue.

The first group of Swedes and Finns left Stockholm Harbor in 1637. The following February, the group reached the Delaware Bay safely. To these hearty travelers, the new country rose like a vision of beauty. They called Cape Henlopen the Point of Paradise. The lands on the west side of the bay and up the river as far as the Falls of Trenton were honorably purchased from the Native Americans, and in honor of their native land, the name of New Sweden was given to the territory.

There were, however, prior claims to the land that was now occupied by the Swedish colony. Stuyvesant regarded New Sweden as part of his dominion, but the Swedes saw not much to be feared from the Dutch, for they were outnumbered ten to one by the Swedes.

The Swedes' fort on the present site of New Castle, Delaware, was seen as an excuse to Stuyvesant for the invasion of New Sweden. In 1655, he led a strike force of 600 troops against the fort. Resistance on the part of the Swedes was useless. Their fortified positions were taken, and the flag of the Neterlands was raised over New Sweden.

NEW YORK

With the restoration of the English monarchy in 1660, Charles II (1630-1685) set about to reclaim the chartered and proprietary governments of the American colonies. In March 1664, he issued two extensive patents for American territory to his brother James (1633-1688), the Duke of York and Albany and later King James II. The first grant included the country from the Kennebec River to the St. Croix River, and the second embraced the whole region between the Connecticut and Delaware rivers.

Without regard to the claims and settlements made by the Dutch West India Company under the authority of the Netherlands, and with no respect for the wishes and interests of the Dutch people who populated Manhattan and the valley of the Hudson River, and ignoring the voice of his own Parliament, Charles II set in motion a land grab that would strip the Netherlands of their North American colonies just as the Netherlands had done to Sweden a decade before.

James himself hurried to secure the benefits and honors that were conceded by the new patents. A fleet of ships was sent out under the command of Richard Nicolls, who the Duke of York had named as governor of what the Dutch still called New Netherland, but which James called "New York" because he was the Duke of York.

On his arrival at New Amsterdam, Nicolls called on Governor Peter

PETER STUYVESANT OF NEW NETHERLAND

Stuyvesant to surrender. The latter was justly angered at the arrogance of the demand, and tried to induce his councilors to declare war. He stormed at them and at the indifferent people of Manhattan with all the passion of a patriot, but they would not fight the British.

Doubtless the Dutch were not lacking in courage, but their property interests were imperiled, and they chose to save their homes at the expense of their patriotism.

On September 8, 1664, New Amsterdam surrendered and New Netherland ceased to exist. The English flag was raised over the fort and New Amsterdam and New Netherland were renamed New York. Two weeks later, Fort Orange on the Hudson was surrendered and renamed Albany in commemoration of the Duke's second title. The Swedish and Dutch settlements on the Delaware also capitulated. England triumphed over her rivals. The conquest was complete. The supremacy of England in central North America was now firmly established. From the northeastern extremity of Maine to the southern limits of Georgia, every mile of the American coast acknowledged the dominion of the English flag and crown.

As soon as the authority of the Dutch was overthrown in New Netherland, a group of Puritans applied to the Duke of York and his governor for the purchase of Native American titles for land purchased earlier by colonists on Newark Bay. The grants to American land made by the English kings frequently overlapped one another, with the second superseding the first or contradicting its provisions.

The Duke of York, in turn, granted the province between the Hudson River and the Delaware to Lord Berkeley and Sir George Carteret, the same noblemen who were already the proprietaries of Carolina.

These factions had adhered to the king's cause during the civil war in England and now received their reward. Their friend Charles II added to their former possessions a second American province of great size and promise. In 1665, Carteret organized the Colony of New Jersey. He named the place after the Isle of Jersey in the English Channel, where he had been governor.

Elizabethtown was made the capital of the new province. Other settlements were abolished on the banks of the Passaic, and Newark was soon founded. Hamlets were planted along the shores of the bay from the present site of Jersey City to Sandy Hook.

In Connecticut, the Dutch had yielded their claims to the English much ear-

JAMES, DUKE OF YORK (LATER JAMES II)

37

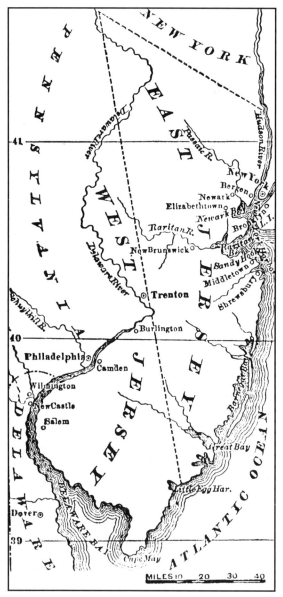

River from Plymouth. The Dutch, however, had previously erected a small trading fort on the river, where Hartford now stands. The consequence of these interfering attempts had been a threatened collision, but it was happily avoided.

Many of the settlers of Plymouth and Massachusetts Bay had been looking for a new home farther west, on the rich lands of the Connecticut. At the head of these was Thomas Hooker and his church. In August 1635, a few pioneers from Dorchester selected a place at Windsor, near the Plymouth trading house. During the same year, John Winthrop, son of the governor of Massachusetts, arrived from England with a commission as governor under Lord Say and Lord Brook, to whom the council of Plymouth had sold a patent for the territory.

Richard Nicolls remained as governor of New York and the Duke of York's other dominions for three years. In 1673, he was superseded by Lord Lovelace, who is remembered for his tyranny and arbitrary rule. He held authority until 1673, when the Dutch, having gone to war with England, sent out a squadron to reclaim their American colony. Amazingly, this expedition was successful, but only at first. New York was actually seized, and the supremacy of Holland was briefly restored in the country between the Connecticut and the Maryland rivers.

lier than in New Netherland. The first house erected in Connecticut was at Windsor, in 1633. It was designed as a trading house, and the materials were transported by boat up the Connecticut

The following year, Charles II was forced by Parliament to negotiate a peace treaty with the Dutch government. However, the treaty contained a clause for the restoration of all conquests made during the war. New York thus reverted to England and the rights of the Duke of York, whatever they were, were again confirmed over the province. The duke made his authority doubly secure by obtaining a new patent confirming the former charter from his brother, the king.

Sir Edmond Andros arrived as governor of New York, but as he attempted to establish his authority, the people resisted him to the verge of insurrection. This state of civil discord remained until 1683, when Andros was superseded by Thomas Dongan, a Catholic.

ENGLISH COURTIERS OF THE COURT OF JAMES II

Under Dongan administration, the form of the government was changed. The assembly of the people was recognized as a part of the colonial management, and all land owners were granted the right to vote.

All the rights and privileges that the people of Massachusetts and Virginia had gained under their charters and the plan of self-government were carefully adopted by the lawmakers of New York in their early constitution. Trial by jury was established, and it was agreed that taxes would not be levied on the people without the consent of the General Assembly. Its regulations protected people from persecution due to their religious beliefs. It also provided that soldiers would not be quartered in people's homes and banned martial law.

In the first year of Dongan's administration, an important treaty was concluded at Albany. In July 1684, the governors of New York and Virginia met with the leaders of the Five Nations of the native Iroquois people (Cayuga, Mohawk, Oneida, Onondaga and Seneca), and the terms of "a lasting peace" were established.

THE EXPANSION OF ENGLISH DOMINANCE

In 1685, Charles II died and his brother, James, Duke of York and "landlord" of New York, ascended to the throne as James II. The new king embraced the English nobility's growing sentiment that it was time to curtail both personal liberties and the tolerance of members of religions other than the official Church of England. The old principles of authoritarian government, which had been avowed and practiced by the kings and queens of the House of Tudor when they ruled England from 1485 to 1603, were again embraced and were acted upon as far as the temper of the English nation would permit.

In this reactionary policy, James II was bolder than his brother. He applied his theory not only to the home administration of England, but to the British colonies in America. As soon as he was seated on the throne, he proceeded to violate the pledges that he had made to his American subjects.

James became an open antagonist of the very government which had been established under his own lieutenants in New York. He abrogated the popular legislature of that province and imposed an odious tax by arbitrary decree on the people. He forbade printing presses and restored all of the old abuses under which the colony had labored and groaned in times past.

Late in 1686, the hated Sir Edmond Andros was sent back to America as governor of all New England. As his deputy, he sent Francis Nicholson to New York and New Jersey to act in his name and under his authority. Governor Dongan was superseded, and New York was converted into a dependency of New England.

With the Revolution of 1688, James II was expelled from the kingdom along with his dependents, partisans and hangers on. The governments of Andros in New England and of Nicholson in New York were immediately overthrown. The governor and his adherents fled the country as Americans hailed the accession of William of Orange (William III) to the throne of England.

With the English Revolution of 1688 and the accession to the throne of King William III (1650-1702) and Queen Mary II (1662-1694) in 1689, the people of Massachusetts hoped for better political conditions. The event, however, did not justify the expectation, as King William didn't want to relinquish the claims of his predecessors in the royal government over the colonies. The policy of sending governors from England was continued, and they were received with disgust by the people.

It is an understatement to say that there was constant variance of interests and views between the citizens and the governors. The General Assembly of Massachusetts insisted that the governor and his councilors should be paid in proportion to the importance of the actual service delivered, but the royal commissioners gave each of them a fixed salary that was frequently out of proportion to their rank and services.

After many years of antagonism, the difficulty was adjusted with a compromise in which the advantage was more on the side of the people.

In 1688, the expulsion of Governor Nicholson from the government occurred following an actual rebellion of the people of New York. The leader of the insurrection was Jacob Leisler, whose action could hardly be condemned by the crown since it was a part of the revolution in England.

However, the new deputy governor, Colonel Sloughter, who was sent out by William and Mary, was induced by Liesler's enemies to have him and his son-in-law arrested, condemned and hanged.

Sloughter's administration began in 1691, but he was soon superseded by Benjamin Fletcher. He held office until the invasion of New York by the French under Governor Frontenac, of Canada, in 1696. Two years later came the Earl of Bellomont, an Anglo-Irish nobleman of excellent character and popular sympathies. His administration lasted for nearly four years and was one of the happiest periods in the history of the colony. His authority was recognized as far as the Housatonic River, and at one time, Massachusetts and New Hampshire were under his jurisdiction, although the colonies of Rhode Island and Connecticut refused to acknowledge his rule.

As an interesting footnote, it was during Bellomont's administration that the coasts and merchant vessels of the eastern and middle colonies were kept in alarm by the ravages of the infamous sea marauder and pirate Captain William Kidd.

Bellomont's benevolent administration ended in 1702, and he was succeeded by the autocratic Lord Cornbury, who soon broke with the popular assembly. Each ensuing legislature resisted his authority, and petitions were circulated for his removal from office.

The councilors chose their own treasurer, refused to make appropriations, cut down the revenue, and vexed the governor with opposition until 1708, when he was not only compelled to retire from office, but had become impoverished and ruined.

The larger colonies of New York and New England were not the only ones to suffer under James II and his arrogant thugs. Rhode Island had been a prosperous colony, full of promise. After the restoration of the colony through the agency of George Baxter, the people secured the confirmation of their charter from King Charles II, and were firmly established as an independent democratic state.

When the despised Andros arrived, he broke the seal of the colony, subverted the government, and appointed an irresponsible council, leaving the fledgling democracy in ruins.

In 1689, however, the people of Rhode Island had their liberties restored. The old democratic institutions were revived and Walter Clark was reelected governor.

Nevertheless, he was fearful of accepting, and an octogenarian Quaker named Henry Bull accepted the task of restoring the old form of government.

South of New York and Pennsylvania, Protestant Virginia and Catholic Maryland were the largest and most prosperous colonies. In Maryland, Leonard Calvert (1606-1647), son of the first Lord Baltimore, the colony's founder, treated the Native Americans near his settlement of St. Mary's with great kindness, and the settlers lived in peace.

The Native Americans and the colonists traded commodities and both communities profited. Indeed, St. Mary's grew into greater prosperity than Jamestown. In 1633, the first assembly of Maryland was convened at St. Mary's, and in 1639, representative government was established in Maryland.

The colony's religious statutes favoring toleration date from 1649. In these freedom of conscience was guaranteed to all. It is remarkable that refuge that was furnished by the Catholic colonists of the Chesapeake Bay area was utilized by Protestants, who had been banished by other Protestants in the neighboring colonies.

The bigotry of the age is further illustrated by the conduct of the Puritan party when they gained the ascendant during the time of the commonwealth in England. The first act of the body was to acknowledge the supremacy of Oliver Cromwell, and the next was to disfranchise and outlaw the Catholics! The result was a civil war.

In 1675, Sir Charles Calvert (1637-1715) became the third Lord Baltimore and succeeded to the estates and titles of his grandfather as governor of Maryland. The population of the colony had now increased to more than 10,000, and the laws of the province were carefully revised on the same liberal principles that had been adopted by the first Lord Baltimore.

The English Revolution of 1688 brought great confusion to the Chesapeake colonists. The deputy of Lord Baltimore hesitated to acknowledge William and Mary as the rightful sovereigns. Meanwhile, however, a rumor was spread by the Protestant party that the Catholics had leagued with the Native Americans for the destruction of all who opposed them. This led to war, and this gave William an opportunity and an excuse to interfere.

In 1691, the charter of Lord Baltimore was arbitrarily taken away and a royal governor appointed over the province. Sir Lionel Copley came to Maryland in 1692, and the old patent as well as the principles on which it had been founded were swept away.

The Church of England was established by law and a system of taxation was invented for its support. Religious toleration was abolished on the very scene of its greatest triumph. It was not until 1715 that Queen Anne would restore the heir of Lord Baltimore to the rights of his ancestors.

In the Carolinas, the Albemarle County colony had William Drummond as its first governor, and the Clarendon County colony was established under the governorship of Sir John Yeamans.

Both settlements flourished, and within a single year, 800 people settled along the Chowan River and the north side of Albemarle Sound. Albemarle County prospered, but the soil of Clarendon County was poor, and in 1671 most of the colonists moved to the mouth of the Ashley River.

As for government, the task was assigned to Sir Ashley Cooper, who appointed the great philosopher John Locke (1632-1704) to prepare a constitution. In 1669, Locke produced a frame of government called the Grand Model. Instead of the practical and people-oriented governments being developed in the other colonies, Locke provided a pompous instrument for the organization of an empire in which there were to be many orders of nobility. These ranged from dukes, earls and marquises to knights, lords, esquires, baronial courts and heraldic ceremony.

Comfortable in his ivory tower, Locke apparently could not conceive of a government tailored to colonists who lived on venison and potatoes and paid their debts with tobacco.

The people of Carolina proceeded to organize for self-government in the simple manner of pioneers. The Grand Model was found impossible to apply and cast aside.

In 1680, the notorious Seth Sothel became deputy governor of the Carolina colony, but he was fortunately captured by pirates, and did not arrive until 1683.

For five years he defrauded and oppressed the people, until he was finally overthrown and sentenced by the General Assembly to disfranchisement and 12 months' banishment.

Old Charleston remained the capital until 1680, when the present city was founded on the peninsula called Oyster Point between the Ashley and Cooper rivers. In 1697, all discrimination against the French immigrants was removed, and in 1695, John Archdale, a distinguished and talented Quaker, was appointed governor.

Under his influence, a law was enacted by which the Huguenots were admitted to full citizenship, and all Christians except the Catholics were enfranchised. This selfish and short-sighted exception was made by the assembly against the governor's will. In 1707, a band of French Huguenots arrived from France. German refugees and peasants from Switzerland also came, and the latter founded New Bern at the mouth of Trent River.

In 1729, seven of the eight proprietaries of the Carolinas sold their entire claims to the provinces to the king. The eighth Lord Carteret would surrender nothing but his right of jurisdiction, reserving his share in the land itself. Also in 1729, the Cape Fear River was made the dividing line between North and South Carolina, and a royal governor was appointed for each of the two colonies.

Early in the eighteenth century, the Church of England was established by law in South Carolina. The status of South Carolina was not to be disturbed for more than 40 years.

QUEEN ANNE'S WAR

Separated by a narrow strip of water that appears on English maps as the English Channel and on French maps as the Pas de Calais, England and France have been rivals, often bitter rivals, since the Middle Ages. The same was true of the citizens of those two lands who transplanted themselves to North America. Nevertheless, throughout the seventeenth century, the North American colonial interests of England and France were separated by enough "wilderness" that the two powers didn't often come to blows.

In North America, the French had dominated the lucrative fur trade, but in 1670, King Charles II (1630-1685) chartered the Hudson Bay Company, which marked the beginning of a major British effort to exploit the resources of the territory north of the St. Lawrence River.

In 1691, the English sent General John Winthrop of Connecticut to Lake Champlain to attack the French at Montreal, but he failed because of a lack of supplies from New York. Another scheme was the invasion of French Canada from Massachusetts, which was only a partial success. It was a source of humiliation to New England that the expedition to Quebec proved to be a failure, but the consequences in other respects were disastrous.

Meanwhile, the indigenous people, who had occupied the land before any Europeans arrived, were also a factor in the balance of power. Indeed, their importance as a third military and political force in what is now the northeastern

ENGLAND'S QUEEN ANNE

United States would be extremely important as events played out in the eighteenth century. Settled along the banks of the Susquehanna River and in the adjacent country, the Five Nations of the Iroquois had been in alliance with Great Britain, and had been a defense to the colonies against the French. Now, however, they became dissatisfied with the English.

In 1697, a treaty was initialed between France and England that called for a mutual restitution of all "the countries, forts and colonies taken by each party during the war."

This peace, however, continued but five short years. It was at the dawn of the eighteenth century that the great European powers came to blows over the issue of who would rule Spain. In May, 1702, England declared war against both France and Spain. Known in Europe as the War of Spanish Succession, the conflict was also called Queen Anne's War, named for the English monarch who was the daughter of James II, and who succeeded William III in 1702. The war involved the French settlements of Canada and the English settlements of Massachusetts, Connecticut and New York. As the war dragged on, Massachusetts planned an attempt to capture Port Royal from the French. In 1707, a fleet bearing 1,000 soldiers sailed from Boston harbor for Acadia. The French colony of Acadia comprised the area that is now part of the Canadian provinces of Nova Scotia and Prince Edward Island, and the northern part of the American state of Maine.

Baron Castin, who commanded the French garrison of Port Royal (now in Nova Scotia), conducted the defense with so much skill and courage that the English were obliged to abandon the undertaking.

Though the Massachusetts forces failed, they decided to try again, and a second contingent was fitted out in 1710. A group of 36 ships with four regiments of troops sailed to Port Royal and began a siege. The garrison was now weakened, and the French commander didn't have the ability of his predecessor. Supplies ran out, and after a defense of eleven days, they surrendered. The English flag was raised over the conquered fortress, and Port Royal was renamed Annapolis, in honor of Queen Anne.

New York participated with New England in the events of Queen Anne's War by sending 1,800 soldiers in an unsuccessful attack on Montreal. The force had proceeded as far as South River, east of Lake George, when news came that the English fleet, which had been expected to cooperate with the American provincial forces in the battle at Quebec, had been sent to Portugal.

The New England force was not strong enough to attempt the capture of the Canadian stronghold, and the New York and New Jersey troops retreated. In 1711, a second expedition was sent forward to the borders of Canada. This time, Sir Hovenden Walker led an English strike force up the St. Lawrence River, but he was overwhelmingly defeated. Meanwhile, the American forces reached Lake George, but when they heard the news of the disaster that befell Walker's fleet, they broke off their attack and returned to their homes.

Queen Anne's War, which had produced a great deal of suffering to the colonies, was terminated by the Treaty of Utrecht in 1713, by which England took control of Acadia.

THE FRENCH AND INDIAN WAR

The English colonies were founded as separate states and generally functioned as such, but by the middle of the eighteenth century, the common interests of the colonies began to prevail over their prejudices, bringing them into a closer union. The French and Indian War from 1754 to 1759 was the most powerful single cause that overcame the spirit of localism and unified all of the colonies.

In 1756, the Seven Years War in Europe pitted England and Prussia against France and its allies, which included Austria, Russia, Saxony, Sweden, and later Spain. The war involved British and French interests in North America as a sort of sideshow, but one that would ultimately have much more far-reaching results than the clash in Europe.

The fertile Ohio River Valley stretches nearly a thousand miles from the Appalachian Mountains to the Mississippi River. England and France each believed this land belonged to them through discovery, exploration, early settlement, long-standing treaties, royal grants and purchase from various Native American tribes. To the English, particularly the colonists of Pennsylvania and Virginia, as well as members of the Ohio Company, the Ohio country was a natural area for expansion by trade and settlement. The French saw it as an economic and defensive link between their colonies of Canada and Louisiana, as well as a buffer to English movements beyond the Appalachians. Both nations aggressively sought the goodwill and assistance of the Native American inhabitants through propaganda and presents distributed by traders and agents. The Native American's concept of land ownership conflicted with European values and culture, and this contributed to their claims to the territory being ignored or forgotten.

French officials, including the Marquis de Duquesne, who became governor-general of New France in 1752, used Native Americans like the Shawnee to harass and hold back English attempts to trade or settle in the area. Other tribes, including many of the Iroquois Confederacy, assisted the English. Duquesne intensified the confrontation by sending detachments of "colony troops" (the *Compagnies Franches de la Marine*) into the disputed area to occupy and fortify key points along the Ohio River and its tributaries.

By the 1740s, English frontiersmen and French trappers were very active as far west as present-day Ohio. Competition and mutual distrust turned to conflict. To make matters worse, and certainly more complicated, England's King George II (1683-1760) issued a land grant to a Virginia company for 5,000 acres in French-claimed territory. Virginia Governor Robert Dinwiddie, Thomas Lee, Lawrence Washington and Augustine (Augustus) Washington now owned a tract north of the Ohio River and adjacent to the Monongahela River that was occupied by 300 French soldiers.

In 1753, as the French began to build a line of forts in this territory, Dinwiddie sent a protest to the French commander. His messenger was the young surveyor son of Augustine Washington. George Washington (1732-1799), who later served as the first president of the United States, made the difficult 1,000-mile trek with an interpreter named Christopher Gist. They returned with bad news. The French would stay and they would evict any Englishman who showed his face.

In 1754, the English came back in force, with George Washington now a lieutenant colonel in the Virginia Militia. Short of a formal declaration of war, the Virginians decided to prosecute their claims by force of arms.

Accordingly, a regiment was raised in Virginia, with a small additional force from South Carolina. Under Washington's command, this force marched in

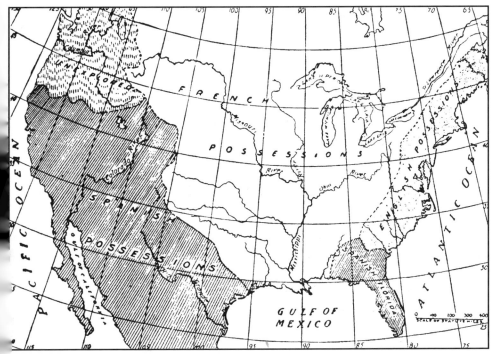

THE NORTH AMERICAN POSSESSIONS OF SPAIN, FRANCE AND ENGLAND (1755-1763).

47

April 1754 toward the Great Meadows, which was within the disputed territories, to expel the French who were camped there. They surrounded an encampment of the enemy, defeated them, and advanced toward the French Fort Duquesne (pronounced *Dew-kane*) on the site of present-day Pittsburgh, Pennsylvania.

With his 400 men, Washington was attacked by 1,500 French troops under General de Villiers. Taking refuge in a hastily-constructed stockade that they called Fort Necessity, the Virginians

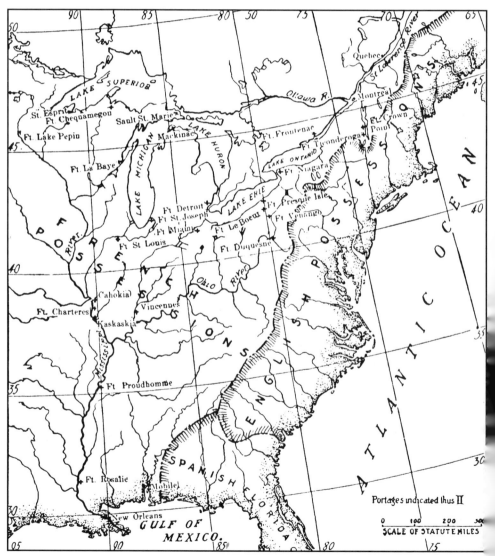

EASTERN NORTH AMERICA IN 1755, HIGHLIGHTING FRENCH FORTS AND CITIES.

fought the French to a stalemate. Unable to win, Washington negotiated a withdrawal under arms.

In 1755, England sent one of its top generals, the Scottish-born Edward Braddock (1695-1755), with 1,500 troops. It was decided that he would lead one of the four expeditions against Fort Duquesne. Brave and highly skilled, Braddock was nevertheless ignorant of Native American warfare. Ignoring Washington, who had two years of valuable, practical experience in the field, Braddock rushed into the midst of the wilderness without proper precautions.

On July 9, the English had pressed as far as the place where Turtle Creek flows into the Monongahela River, only 12 miles from their objective at Fort Duquesne. When ambushed by the French and Native Americans, Braddock responded as if he were pitted against a regular European army.

He undauntedly stood their attack, but had no means of reaching the enemy, who were firing from the thick woods. He sought to preserve a regular order of battle, but being fair marks for the Native American gun or arrow, Braddock's troops suffered heavy casualties. Of the officers on horseback, Washington alone escaped unhurt. Braddock himself was mortally wounded, and the English troops, unfamiliar with the guerrilla tactics of North American warfare, fled in confusion while Washington cov-

GEORGE WASHINGTON'S VIRGINIA TROOPS ATTACK THE FRENCH NEAR FORT DUQUESNE.

ered their retreat with the provincial troops.

The defeat was total. The entire western frontier of Virginia's claim was open to future attacks by the French and Native Americans.

Meanwhile, in the northern colonies, 4,000 troops had been assembled at the end of June 1755 under General William Johnson of New York. At Albany, they were joined by a group of Mohawks, under Chief Hendrick. The army arrived at the south end of Lake George, about 50 miles north of Albany, by the latter part of August. Here, they received word that 2,000 French troops under the command of Baron Dieskau had arrived near Lake Champlain, and were marching toward Fort Edward, to destroy the provisions and military supplies there.

A detachment of 1,200 troops, commanded by Colonel Ephraim Williams of Deerfield, Massachusetts, was sent to intercept the French and save the fort. Dieskau, however, succeeded in routing this force by drawing them into an ambush. Colonel Williams and Hendrick were among the slain. The troops retreated and joined the main body a troops at Lake George. Here they awaited the approach of their assailants, who were rendered more formidable by success.

Johnson was prepared, and the Dieskau's attack was vigorously repulsed. The French retreated with the English colonists in hot pursuit. Dieskau was mortally wounded and died soon after. The Battle of Lake George elevated the mood of the English in the wake of the defeat of Braddock.

Meanwhile, a force of 3,000 attacked the French in Nova Scotia. Sailing from Boston in May 1755, they landed in the Bay of Fundy and were joined by 300 British troops with artillery. They captured the French Fort Beau Sejour after a bombardment of five days. General Monckton, advancing farther into the country, took other French forts and disarmed the inhabitants. Thus, with the loss of only three men, the English gained the whole of Nova Scotia.

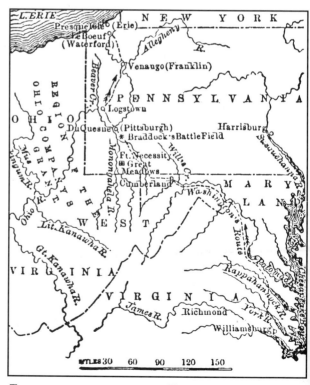

THE SOUTHERN FRONT OF THE FRENCH AND INDIAN WAR.

New York Governor William Shirley (1694-1771) led an attack against the French in the Niagara region in late 1755, but he found the season was too far advanced for crossing Lake Ontario.

Although a state of warfare had existed for two years in the colonies, it was not until 1756 that war was formally declared between France and England in what would be the Seven Years War. This marked a reversal of the fortunes enjoyed by the English in the wake of the Braddock fiasco. At attempted attack on Louisburg, the capital of the Island of Cape Breton that was fortified with great care and expense by the French, was broken off without success in 1757, while smaller skirmishes inland also met with failure.

In August 1757, French forces under General Marquis Louis Joseph de Montcalm (1712-1759) seized the occasion to make a descent on Fort William Henry on the north shore of Lake George. After a gallant defense of six days, the garrison surrendered, thus giving Montcalm the command of the lakes and the western frontier.

In the European theater of the conflict, the English were also being mauled by French forces, but reversal of

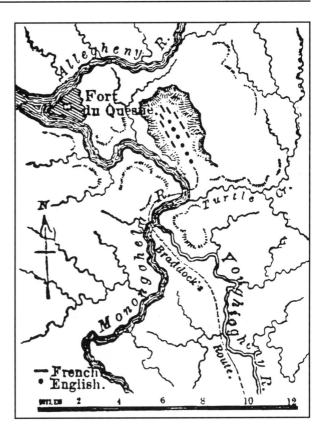

THE SCENE OF BRADDOCK'S DEFEAT IN 1755.

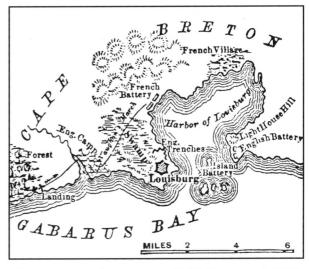

FRANCE WON AT LOUISBURG IN 1757, ENGLAND IN 1758.

England's fortune (or lack thereof) would soon come at the hands of a confident and ingenious manager. In 1758, King George II picked William Pitt (1708-1778), the Earl of Chatham, as his prime minister. Pitt adopted a bold and aggressive plan of action on all fronts. As far as the conflict in North America was concerned, his best move was to assign the young but brilliant General James Wolfe (1727-1759) to command the English forces against the French.

A three-pronged offensive was undertaken. The first was against Louisburg, the second was against Ticonderoga, north of Lake George, and the third was against Fort Duquesne. The attack on Louisburg involved 20 ships of the

THE DEATH OF GENERAL EDWARD BRADDOCK NEAR FORT DUQUESNE ON JULY 9, 1755.

line, 18 frigates and an army of 14,000 under the command of Brigadier General Amherst.

The fortress surrendered on July 26, 1758, with nearly 6,000 prisoners, and Isle Royal, St. Johns and Cape Breton also fell into the hands of the British. The latter were now the masters of the coast, from the St. Lawrence to Nova Scotia, and were able to obstruct the lines of communications between France and New France (Canada).

Under General James Abercrombie (1706-1781), the July expedition against Ticonderoga, on the western shore of Lake Champlain, was a failure, and as such, this battle was the principal exception to the general tide of success on the part of the English. In the attack against the fort, nearly 2,000 men were killed or wounded.

Some amends were made for this defeat by the taking of Fort Frontenac, on the western shore of the outlet of Lake Ontario.

The attack against Fort Duquesne was assigned to an 8,000-man force under General Forbes, but the fort was deserted by the French garrison the evening before the arrival of the English army. The place was then named Pittsburgh in honor of William Pitt.

THE FRENCH BESIEGED AND CAPTURED FORT WILLIAM HENRY IN AUGUST 1757.

ENGLISH GENERAL JAMES WOLFE

The objective of the campaign of 1759 was the entire conquest of Canada. Three powerful English armies would enter the country by different routes and simultaneously attack the French strongholds at Ticonderoga, Crown Point, Niagara and Quebec. In July, the British captured Fort Ticonderoga and defeated the French in a bloody contest at Fort Niagara. Crown Point was abandoned by the French in September before the arrival of the English.

Meanwhile, however, the capture of the city of Quebec was seen as the cornerstone of the entire campaign. The September 1759 climax to the war would also be a contest between two of the most important and highly regarded European military commanders to serve in North America. General Wolfe was in command of the English attacking forces, while the defending French forces were commanded by General Marquis Louis Joseph de Montcalm.

The English had already succeeded in sealing off the St. Lawrence to prevent supplies from coming into Quebec, but Montcalm remained confident that the heavily fortified city was impregnable. The fortifications had, after all, thwarted English attacks in 1690 and 1716.

However, the English surprised the French by scaling the high cliffs west of Quebec and overwhelming its defenders. Wolfe himself was killed in the assault, but his plan worked, and his

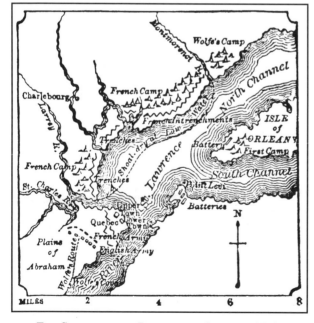

THE SCENE OF THE BATTLE FOR QUEBEC, 1759.

forces were able to seize the capital of New France. Montcalm was also killed, making the contest unique in that both commanding generals died while actually leading their troops in battle.

The French defeat at Quebec assured England of a superpower status and also gave it unquestioned supremacy over most of the area of North America that had already been settled by Europeans. This predominance was destined to be short-lived, however, as unrest was already brewing in the 13 colonies to the south of the St. Lawrence River.

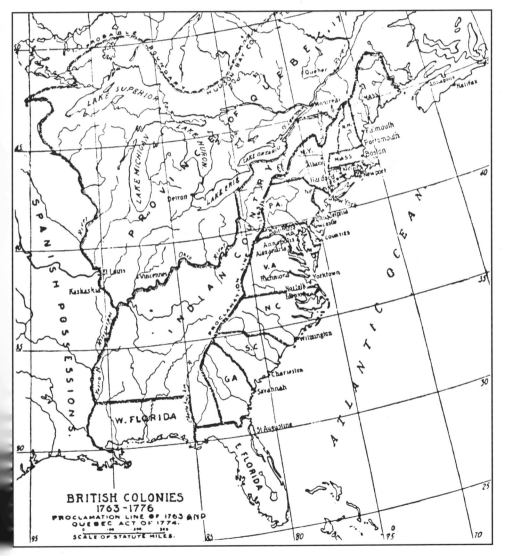

BRITISH COLONIES
1763-1776
PROCLAMATION LINE OF 1763 AND
QUEBEC ACT OF 1774.
SCALE OF STATUTE MILES.

AFTER A CENTURY OF STRUGGLE, THE BRITISH DOMINATED THIS REALM FOR ONLY 13 YEARS.

WHERE TO GO

This section is designed as your guide to parks, historic sites, museums and interpretive centers in the United States and its territories where you can go to see what life was like in the historical period covered by *Our Colonial Period.*

At these sites, you can see where many of the events in the book actually took place, or view exhibits relating to the everyday lives of the people, both Native and European, who lived and worked in North America in the period from 1607 to 1770 and beyond.

1. Acadia National Park
PO Box 177
Bar Harbor, ME 04609
(207) 288-3338

This scenic park includes Mount Desert Island, discovered by Samuel Champlain in 1604, and the site of a short-lived French Jesuit settlement in 1613.

2. Maine Maritime Museum
263 Washington Street
Bath, ME 04530
(207) 443-1316

The focus of the 10-acre site is the maritime history of Maine since 1607, with an emphasis upon nineteenth century sailing ships. It includes two former shipyards; the restored Grand Banks schooner *Sherman Zwicker*; the apprentice shop, where traditional boat construction and repair skills are still taught; and a collection of small craft used along Maine's coast and waterways.

3. Sewell House
963 Washington Street
Bath, ME 04530
(207) 443-1316

Associated with the Maine Maritime Museum, the Sewell House features a large collection of marine paintings, sailor's artifacts and a children's room.

4. Wilson Museum
Perkins Street
Castine, ME 04421
(207) 326-8753

The museum features prehistoric materials from Europe, Africa and the Americas; Indian artifacts; colonial items; the John Perkins House, a pre-Revolutionary War building, restored and furnished with period pieces; a blacksmith shop; and a hearse house.

5. Pownalborough Courthouse
West of Dresden on SR 128, ME 04342
(207) 737-2504

The only pre-Revolutionary War courthouse in the state, it includes a furnished courtroom, the judges' chambers, bedrooms, a kitchen, a tavern, a parlor and displays of antique tools and machinery.

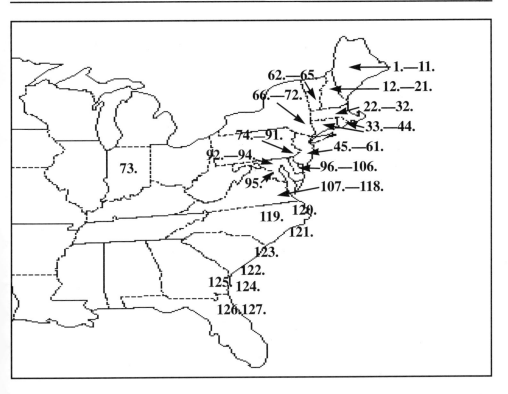

The map contains the following labels:

- 1.—11.
- 12.—21.
- 22.—32.
- 33.—44.
- 45.—61.
- 62.—65
- 66.—72.
- 73.
- 74.—91.
- 92.—94.
- 95.
- 96.—106.
- 107.—118.
- 119.
- 120.
- 121.
- 122.
- 123.
- 124.
- 125.
- 126.127.

6. Kittery Historical and Naval Museum

Rogers Road
North of Junction US 1 and SR 236
Kittery, ME 03904
(207) 439-3080

The museum portrays the shipbuilding heritage of Kittery and other early towns. Various models, artifacts and manuscripts describe more than 300 years of Maine history with a special emphasis on the Portsmouth Naval Shipyard.

7. Colonial Pemaquid State Historical Site

off SR 130
Pemaquid Point, ME 04558
(207) 677-2423

The museum displays artifacts excavated from the area, as well as the site of an English settlement attempted in the early seventeenth century.

8. Fort William Henry State Historical Site

Pemaquid Beach, ME 04558
(207) 677-2423

The fort was constructed by the British in 1692 and captured and destroyed by the French only four years later. Fort Frederick was then built on the same site in 1729 and leveled by the colonists during the American Revolution. A reproduction has been built on the original foundation.

9. Tate House
1270 Westbrook Street
Portland, ME 04102
(207) 774-9781

The Tate House is a three story gambrel-roofed house built in 1755 for George Tate, the mast agent for the British Crown, and furnished with eighteenth century furnishings.

10. Acadian Village
5 miles north on US 1
Van Buren, ME 04785
(207) 868-2691

The village includes a general store, a country schoolhouse, a blacksmith shop, a chapel, a museum and several homes, all depicting mid-eighteenth century life in the St. John Valley.

11. Old York Historical Society
140 Lindsay Road
York, ME 03909
(207) 363-4974

The historical society maintains restored buildings in several locations that represent life in York, including: the Elizabeth Perkins House (1732), the Emerson-Wilcox House (c. 1742), the Jefferd's Tavern (1750), the John Hancock Warehouse, the Old Gaol Museum (1719) and the Old Schoolhouse (1745).

12. Old Fort Number Four
SR 11, 1/2 mile west of Junction SR 12, 1 mile east of I-91, exit 7
Charlestown, NH 03603
(603) 826-5700

Old Fort Number Four is a reconstruction of the 1744 fortified village of Charlestown, with furnishings and craft demonstrations depicting eighteenth century frontier life.

13. Woodman Institute
182-192 Central Avenue
Dover, NH 03820
(603) 742-1038

The Woodman Institute features three display buildings, including the hand-hewn Damm Garrison House (1682), which is furnished with early American cooking utensils, farm tools, clothing and furniture.

14. Gilman Garrison House
12 Water Street
Exeter, NH 03833
(603) 436-3205

Built in the late seventeenth century as a fortified house, the house was remodeled in the eighteenth century and is furnished with seventeenth and eighteenth century pieces.

15. Heritage — New Hampshire
1/2 mile north of Junction US 302 on SR 16
Glen, NH 03838
(603) 383-9776

Heritage — New Hampshire uses an audiovisual presentation to trace 300 years of New Hampshire history, beginning with the voyage from England on a sailing ship and ending with a simulated train ride through Crawford Notch.

16. Portsmouth Trail
Chamber of Commerce
500 Market Street
Portsmouth, NH 03801
(603) 436-1118

Tickets and tour maps are available at the Chamber of Commerce. The tour of historic buildings includes:
the Governor John Langdon House (1784), the John Paul Jones House (1758), the Moffatt-Ladd House (1763), the Rundlet-May House (1807), the Warner House (1716) and the Wentworth-Gardner House (1760).

17. Prescott Park
105 Marcy Street
Portsmouth, NH 03801
(603) 431-8748

The park contains gardens, fountains, a fishing pier, picnic area and two old warehouses, including the Sheafe Warehouse (1705), which now houses the Folk Art Museum.

18. Strawberry Banke Museum
10 acres bounded by Marcy, State, Washington and Hancock streets
Portsmouth, NH 03801
(603) 433-1100

The museum preserves the historic waterfront neighborhood, including 35 buildings that date from 1695 to 1820 and are in various stages of restoration and adaptation.

19. Wentworth-Coolidge Mansion
Little Harbor Road
Portsmouth, NH 03801

Built around 1695, the mansion was the official residence of the first Royal Governor, Benning Wentworth, from 1741 to 1766.

20. Frye's Measure Mill
1 1/2 miles north on SR 31
(Left after crossing the railroad tracks and bridge at the fork,
then 1 1/2 miles to the mill.)
Wilton, NH 03806
(603) 654-6581

Portions of the mill date from 1750, when the site was a smithy. In the 1850s, hand card machinery was imported from England. The tour and demonstrations include the carding of wool, the preparation of fleece for spinning, the use of water-driven machinery, and the making of Shaker boxes.

21. Hampshire Pewter Company
9 Mill Street
Wolfeboro, NH 03894
(603) 569-4944

Visitors receive free factory tours of the only firm in the country to mix and use "the Queen's Metal." The company uses sixteenth century techniques to make pewter hollowware and table top accessories.

22. Boston National Historical Park
Charlestown Navy Yard, Boston, MA 02129
(617) 242-5642

The Boston National Historical Park is an association of a number of sites that together give the visitor a coherent view of the city's role in the nation's history. Most of the historic sites are connected by the Freedom Trail, and each brings to life the American ideals of freedom of speech, religion, government and self-determination.

23. Harvard University
Harvard Information Center
1350 Massachusetts Avenue
Cambridge, MA 02138
(617) 495-1573

One of the oldest universities in the country, Harvard was founded in 1636. The historic campus includes Massachusetts Hall (1720), University Hall (1813) and the late nineteenth century Sever Hall, as well as several major museums.

24. Historic Deerfield
Deerfield, MA 01342
(413) 774-5581

This complex of 12 historic homes includes: the Allen House (1720), the Ashley House, the Barnard Tavern (early nineteenth century), the Dwight House (1725), the Ebenezer Hinsdale and Anna Williams House (restored to its 1813-1838 appearance), the Frary House (eighteenth century, then restored in 1890), the Helen Geier Flynt Textile Museum, the Henry Needham Flynt Silver and Metalware Collection, the Sheldon-Hawkes House, the Stebbins House, the Wells-Thorn House (1725 to 1850 period rooms) and the Wright House (1824).

25. Abbot Hall
Washington Square
Marblehead, MA 01945
(617) 631-0000

Abbot Hall exhibits the 1684 deed recording the purchase of the peninsula from the Native Americans, as well as the original "Spirit of '76" painted in 1876 by A.M. Willard.

26. St. Michael's Church
26 Pleasant Street
Marblehead, MA 01945
(617) 631-0657

Built in 1714 with materials imported from England, the church is one of the oldest Episcopal churches in America. Guided tours are available by appointment.

27. The Pilgrim Path and Plymouth Rock
Plymouth Information Center
130 Water Street
Plymouth, MA 02360
(508) 747-7525 or (800) USA-1620

The Pilgrim Path features more than 20 sites on a self guided walking tour. Plymouth Rock, the site where the Pilgrims first set foot on American soil in December 1620, is also included.

28. Burial Hill
Town Square
Plymouth, MA 02360

The hill was the site of a fort built in 1622, a watchtower built in 1643 and the burial place of Governor William

Bradford. On every Friday in August, citizens reenact the church service of the 51 survivors of their first winter of 1620-1621.

29. *Mayflower II*
State Pier
Plymouth, MA 02360
(508) 746-1622

Mayflower II is a reproduction of the type of ship that brought the Pilgrims to the New World in the seventeenth century. It features costumed guides who portray the passengers and crew, as well as exhibits showing the history of the *Mayflower*.

30. The Plimoth Plantation
Plimoth Plantation Highway
Exit 4 off SR 3
Plymouth, MA 02360
(508) 746-1622

The plantation is a living history museum of seventeenth century Plymouth, with costumed interpreters portraying the residents of the colony. Activities include planting, house building, harvesting, preparing food, preserving food and militia drills.

31. Salem Maritime
National Historic Site
Custom House, Derby Street
Salem, MA 01970
(508)745-1470

The Salem Maritime National Historic Site is located on Derby Street, Salem, MA, 20 miles northeast of Boston. Here, on the old waterfront, visitors can see the once busy wharves, the warehouses, the Custom House, the Scale House, the West India Goods Store, the Derby House, the Hawkes House, the Narbonne-Hale House and the Lighthouse on Derby Wharf.

32. Salem Witch Museum
Washington Square
Salem, MA 01970
(508) 744-1692

Opposite the Salem Common, the museum depicts the witch trials of 1692. A dramatic audiovisual presentation is shown every half hour.

33. Ancient Burying Ground
60 Gold Street
Hartford, CT 06103
(203) 249-5631

This was Hartford's only cemetery until 1803. The oldest gravestone dates from 1636. The Center Church (1807) features six Tiffany windows. Tours are available by appointment only.

34. The Green
Greater New Haven Convention and Visitor's Bureau
1 Long Wharf Drive, Suite 7
New Haven, CT 06511
(203) 777-8550 or (800) 332-7829

In 1638, New Haven was laid out by the Puritans in nine equal squares. The 16-acre central square, or green, was reserved for the public and remains as plotted by the original settlers. The only buildings that still stand on the green are the three churches on Temple Street, which were all built around 1815.

35. Old New-Gate Prison
Newgate Road
East Granby, CT 06026
(203) 653-3563

Colonial America's first copper mine began operations in 1707. During the Revolutionary War, it was converted into a prison for Tories and others, and in 1776, it became the first state prison in the nation. Visitors can see the underground caverns, the old prison buildings, and restored guardhouse.   .

36. Tapping Reeve House and Law School
South Street
Litchfield, CT 06759
(203) 567-4501

The 1774 house contains furniture and other items dating from 1750 to 1825. Tapping Reeve founded the nation's first law school in 1784.

37. Yale University
New Haven, CT 06520
(203) 432-2300

Yale University was named for Elihu Yale, an East India trader and generous donor. Founded in Bransford, it held its first classes in Killingsworth in 1701. It moved to Old Saybrook in 1707 and then to New Haven in 1716. The campus includes Connecticut Hall (1752), where Nathan Hale lived and studied; the Memorial Quadrangle, a block of dormitories designed in the Gothic style; the Beinecke Rare Book and Manuscript Library; the Peabody Museum of Natural History; the Sterling Memorial Library; the Woolsey Hall; the Yale Center for British Art; the Yale Collection of Musical Instruments; and the Yale University Art Gallery.

38. Buttolph-Williams House
Broad and Marsh Streets
Wethersfield, CT 06109
(203) 529-0460 / 247-8996

Built in 1692, the Buttolph-Williams House is the oldest restored house in Wethersfield. The colonial lifestyle is reflected in the period furnishings. Wethersfield, along with Windsor, claims to be the oldest permanent English settlement in Connecticut. Many of the other structures in town that were constructed prior to 1800 are marked with the date of construction and the names of the original owners.

39. Hunter House
54 Washington Street
Newport, RI 02840
(401) 847-1000

Built in 1748 by Jonathan Nichols, the Deputy Governor of Rhode Island, the restored house is an outstanding example of colonial architecture. It features eighteenth century furniture, paneling, paintings, silver and a colonial garden. It served as the headquarters of Admiral de Ternay, the commander of the French naval forces, during the Revolutionary War.

40. Redwood Library and Athenaeum
50 Bellevue Drive
Newport, RI 02840
(401) 847-0292

Built between 1748 and 1750, the library contains many old and valuable books. It also has a collection of eighteenth and nineteenth century portraits, including seven by Gilbert Stuart.

41. Touro Synagogue
National Historic Site
85 Touro Street
Newport, RI 02840
(401) 847-4794

Built in 1763, this is the oldest synagogue in the nation. The interior is considered to be an architectural masterpiece. It is closed on holy days except for services. Call ahead for schedules.

42. Trinity Church
Queen Anne Square
Newport, RI 02840
(401) 846-0660

The Trinity Church has been in continuous use since it was built in 1726. The spire is still topped with the golden bishop's mitre of the Church of England. The interior features Tiffany windows, a three-tiered wineglass pulpit, the original chandeliers and an organ tested by Handel.

43. Wanton-Lyman-Hazard House
17 Broadway
Newport, RI 02840
(401) 846-0813

This restored 1675 house is one of the finest examples of Jacobean architecture in New England. Home of Colonial governors, it was also the site of the Stamp Act Riot of 1765. The grounds also feature a colonial garden.

44. Slater Mill Historic Site
Roosevelt Avenue
Pawtucket, RI 02865
(401) 725-8638

This cotton mill has been restored to its early nineteenth century appearance to show the development of factory production and life in a nineteenth century industrial village. Guided tours include the Sylvanus Brown House (1758), where weaving and hand spinning are demonstrated; the Slater Mill (1793); and the Wilkinson Mill (1810).

45. Bridgeton City Park
West Commerce Street and Mayor Aitken Drive
Bridgeton, NJ 08302
(609) 455-3230

The park covers 1,100 acres and includes facilities for boating, fishing and swimming; a recreation center; the Nail Mill Museum, a diverse collection of memorabilia and local history items; and the New Sweden Farmstead Museum, a reproduction of seventeenth century buildings typical of the early Swedish settlements of the area.

46. Bard-How House
453 High Street
Burlington, NJ 08016
(609) 386-4773

Built in 1740, the restored building houses period furnishings, clocks and other accessories.

47. Camden County Historical Society
Park Boulevard at Euclid Avenue
Camden, NJ 08103
(609) 964-3333

The society's museum contains period furniture, antique glass, toys, fire-fighting equipment, eighteenth and nineteenth century newspapers, and an original Victor Talking Machine. The grounds also include Pomona Hall (1726), which is furnished with period pieces.

48. Leamings's Run Gardens and Colonial Farm
1/2 mile west of Garden State Parkway, Exit 13, then 1 mile north on US 9
Cape May Court House, NJ 08210
(609) 465-5871

This attraction features 25 gardens, each with its own theme, as well as a reconstructed colonial farm, which contains a one-room log cabin depicting seventeenth century life.

49. Steuben House State Historic Site (Ackerman-Zabriskie-Steuben House)
1209 Main Street
Hackensack, NJ 07601
(201) 487-1739

The 1713 house displays the museum collection of the Bergen County Historical Society and Jersey Dutch furnishings dating from 1650-1850. The house was also General George Washington's headquarters in 1780.

50. Indian King Tavern House Museum
233 Kings Highway
Haddonfield, NJ 08033
(609) 429-6792

Built around 1750, the building is furnished with period pieces and contains many historic artifacts.

51. Museum of Early Trades and Crafts
Main Street and Green Village Road
Madison, NJ 07940
(201) 377-2982

The museum displays and explains tools and techniques of trades and crafts from the late seventeenth century to 1850. It includes implements used by cobblers, coopers, tinsmiths, wheelwrights, leather workers and others.

52. Marlpit Hall
137 Kings Highway
Middletown, NJ 07748
(908) 462-1466

Originally built as a one-room Dutch cottage in 1685, the home was enlarged in the English style about 1740, and today the restored building and collection of furnishings display life in Middletown over several generations.

53. The Morris Museum
2 1/2 miles east on CR 510 at
Normandy Heights and Columbia roads
Morristown, NJ 07960
(201) 538-0454

The museum includes: galleries on natural and earth sciences, as well as decorative and fine arts; a 5,000-foot gallery
featuring changing national and interna-
tional exhibits; the Five Senses Gallery,
designed for children under age 6; and
exhibits on Native Americans and colonial life.

54. New Jersey Museum of Agriculture
(Off US 1 on College Farm Road
on the Cook College campus at
Rutgers)
New Brunswick, NJ 08903
(908) 249-2077

The museum depicts the history of agricultural science, from the Native
Americans to the present, including
exhibits on everyday life in colonial
New Jersey.

55. The Spy House Museum
119 Port Monmouth Road
Port Monmouth, NJ 07758
(908) 787-1807

This 1663 building has evolved from a
one room cabin to a large house. The
museum, a hands-on learning center,
illustrates the lifestyle of the early settlers and Native Americans, the water-
man trades, and the heritage of the
bayshore.

56. Dey Mansion
199 Totowa Road
Preakness Valley Park, NJ 07470
(201) 696-1776

The 1740 brick and brownstone
Georgian house displays antiques and
items from the eighteenth century in
both the detached kitchen and main
house. General George Washington also
used the house for his headquarters in
July, October and November of 1780.

57. Ringwood State Park
2 1/2 miles north via Skyland Drive,
CR 511 and Sloatsburg Road
Ringwood, NJ 07456
(201) 962-7031

Found here, Ringwood Manor's third
floor contains exhibits showing the history of the iron industry from 1740 to
the 1920s.

58. Somers Mansion
1000 Shore Road
Somers Point, NJ 08244
(609) 927-2212

Built around 1725 by Richard Somers,
the house features eighteenth century
antiques, a textile collection of quilts,
coverlets and samplers, and architectural details of the interior woodwork dec-
orated with heart-shaped perforations.

59. Old Dutch Parsonage State Historic Site
65 Washington Place
Somerville, NJ 08876
(908) 725-1015

Built in 1751, the site contains exhibits featuring local history and early American crafts and lifestyles.

60. Trent House
15 Market Street
Trenton, NJ 08611
(609) 989-3027

Built in 1719, the Trent House has been the home of many prominent men, including the first colonial governor of New Jersey, Lewis Morris. The home is furnished with period pieces, including curtains and copies of old fabrics.

61. Cape May County
Historical Museum
504 Route 9, R.D. #1
Cape May Court House, NJ 08210
(609) 465-3535

The history museum is located in the John Holmes House (c. 1780). The collections include Native American artifacts, the colonial kitchen, Victoriana, whaling, military items, and maritime history.

62. Bennington
Chamber of Commerce
Veterans Memorial Drive
Bennington, VT 05201

The restored Old First Church has been restored to its early 1700s appearance. Its cemetery contains the graves of soldiers who died in the Battle of Bennington in 1777 and the poet Robert Frost. The Bennington Museum displays a collection of Grandma Moses paintings and Early American memora-

bilia. It also operates the restored Peter Matteson Tavern in Shaftsbury.

63. Vermont State Capitol
State Street
Montpelier, VT

The capitol building is an impressive Doric style. Built of Barre granite, the structure features a gilded dome surmounted by a statue of Ceres, the goddess of agriculture. Inside stands a brass cannon captured from the Hessians in the Battle of Bennington (1777) and a statue of Ethan Allen.

64. The Vermont Museum
Pavilion Office Building
109 State Street
Montpelier, VT
(802) 828-2291

The museum traces the history of Vermont, from the Native Americans to the present. Changing exhibitions feature different historical themes.

65. Shelburne Museum and
Heritage Park
US 7
Shelburne, VT
(802) 985-3344

A collection of 37 restored buildings, many dismantled and moved to the park, housing collections of art, artifacts and memorabilia depicting early New England life. Some of the structures are furnished eighteenth and nineteenth century houses, a jail, country store, schoolhouse, stagecoach inn, apothecary, blacksmith shop and railroad depot.

Other attractions include a double lane covered bridge, round barn, locomotive and private car, a model circus parade more than 500 feet long and the 1906 sidewheeler S.S. *Ticonderoga.* The museum features many varied collections focusing upon Americana.

66. Dutch Homes on the Hudson
New York Division of Tourism
1 Commerce Plaza
Albany, NY 12245

Houses of the early Dutch settlers and their descendants are to be found throughout the Hudson River Valley.

67. The Erie Canal
NY Department of Transportation
1220 Washington Avenue
Albany, NY 12232

Mules and horses towed wooden barges along the 363 mile long canal that linked Albany with Buffalo. *"Clinton's Folly"* speeded trade and settlement of the old northwest. The original locks can be seen at Fort Hunter, located west of Amsterdam, and at Lockport. Near Rome is the Oriskany Battlefield, scene of a Revolutionary War battle.

68. Museum Village in Orange County
Museum Village Road
Monroe, NY 10950

The village's 30 buildings portray the era of homespun craft shops and emerging industries. Craft demonstrations show broom-making, weaving, printing, blacksmithing and pottery making.

69. Fort Stanwix National Monument
112 East Park Street
Rome, NY 13440
(315) 336-2090

Originally built in 1758, Fort Stanwix has been almost completely reconstructed to its 1777 appearance. It features a storehouse, bombproof barracks and casemates. Exhibits at the museum depict the history of the upper Mohawk Valley. The park is on a tour and living history schedule for most of the year.

70. Fort Ticonderoga
Route 74
Ticonderoga, NY 12883

Reconstructed to the original 1755 French plans, the fort features a parade ground, bastions, barracks, ramparts, a museum and a well-marked battlefield around the fort.
The fort was first called Fort Carillon by the French and renamed Ticonderoga after its capture in 1759 by the British. During the Revolution, the fort fell to Ethan Allen's Green Mountain Boys.

71. New York Historical Society
170 Central Park West at 77th Street
New York, NY
(212) 873-3400

The historical society houses a museum, print room and reference library. Its collections focus upon American history, New York history, American fine arts and the decorative arts.

72. New York Public Library
42nd Street and Fifth Avenue
New York, NY
(212) 930-0800

The library features more than five million volumes in its research library, including 21 specialized collections of American history, art, periodicals, and Slavic, Jewish and Oriental literature.

73. Vincennes
Vincennes Chamber of Commerce
417 Busseron Street
Vincennes, IN 47591

The city of Vincennes, founded as a French trading post in 1683 and renamed Fort Sackville by the British in 1763, was captured by George Rogers Clark during the Revolutionary War. From 1800 to 1813, the area was governed from the Indiana Territorial Capitol. Near the capitol building is a reconstruction of the newspaper office that held Indiana's first press. President William Henry Harrison (1841) built Grouseland, which now exhibits family portraits and furnishings, while he was the territorial governor.

74. Daniel Boone Homestead
9 miles east of Reading on US 422, (then 1 mile north on Daniel Boone Road.)
Baumstown, PA
(610) 582-4900

The 579-acre restored Boone Homestead features the original 10-room stone house built by the Boone family in 1730. The home is furnished with mid-eighteenth century Pennsylvania furniture. Also on the grounds are a restored blacksmith shop, a sawmill, a barn, the Bertolet Log House (1730), picnic and hiking areas, and a visitor center.

75. Old Bedford Village
1 mile north on US 220,
3/4 mile south of the Pennsylvania Turnpike, Exit 11
Bedford, PA 15522
(800) 238-4347 or (814) 623-1156

This is a 40 building reproduction of a village from the 1750-1850 period. Crafts demonstrated include tinsmithing, broom making, leather making, quilting, spinning, weaving and woodworking. Numerous special events are also held here.

76. The Chester County Historical Society
225 North High Street
West Chester, PA
(610) 692-4800

The historical society displays early American furniture and decorative arts, including clocks, ceramics, crystal and silver. The changing exhibits feature clothing, textiles, dolls and ceramics. It also maintains a research library which focuses upon genealogy and area history.

77. Eighteenth-Century Industrial Quarter
459 Old York Road
Bethlehem, PA 18018
(800) 360-8687 or (610) 868-1513

The Industrial Quarter buildings include: a tannery (1761); the Springhouse (1764); the Luchenbach Mill (1869); and the Waterworks (1762), the first municipal pumping system in the Colonies. Colonial trades are demonstrated by artisans.

78. Lycoming County Historical Museum
858 West Fourth Street
Williamsport, PA
(717) 326-3326

The museum features artifacts ranging from 10,000 BC and the early Native American cultures to the arrival of the European settlers. Among the exhibits are a blacksmith shop, a carpenter shop, a Victorian parlor, a gristmill and a Shempp toy train collection.

79. Moravian Museum of Bethlehem
66 West Church Street
Bethlehem, PA 18018
(610) 867-0173

The museum is located in the Gemein Haus (1741), the oldest building in Bethlehem, and displays silver, musical instruments, seminary art, needlework, Moravian furniture and clocks.

80. Sun Inn
564 Main Street
Bethlehem, PA 18017
(215) 866-1758

The Sun Inn, established in 1758 as a way station for Colonial statesmen like George Washington, the Marquis de Lafayette and John Adams, is fully restored and furnished in period.

81. Thomas Massey House
1 mile south of SR 3 on Lawrence Road at Springhouse Road
Broomall, PA 19008
(610) 353-3644

Built in 1696, the house is one of the oldest English Quaker homes in Pennsylvania. It has been restored to its original condition and features period furnishings and implements.

82. Harriton House
1 1/4 miles north of US 30 on Morris Avenue, (then 1/2 mile west on Old Gulph Road, then north on Harriton Road to the entrance.)
Bryn Mawr, PA 19010
(610) 525-0201

Built in 1704, the two-story stone house was the home of Charles Thomson, secretary of the Continental Congress. The house has been restored and contains some of its original furnishings.

83. Peter Wentz Farmstead
3/10 mile southeast of Junction SR 73 and 363
Center Point, PA 19474
(610) 584-5104

This eighteenth century working farm features a Georgian-style mansion furnished in period, livestock, a German kitchen garden, apple orchards, craft and farming demonstrations, and a slide presentation. The house was also used twice as George Washington's head-quarters during the Revolutionary War.

84. Wright's Ferry Mansion
2nd and Cherry Streets
Columbia, PA 17512
(717) 684-4325

This 1738 colonial home of Susanna Wright, a literary Quaker, contains a collection of early eighteenth century Philadelphia furniture, reflecting life in a Pennsylvania Quaker household prior to 1750.

85. Newlin Mill Park
1 1/2 miles east on US 1
Concordville, PA 19331
(610) 459-2359

The 150-acre park features a restored gristmill (1704), a miller's house (1739), a blacksmith shop, a spring-house and a log cabin.

86. Cornwall Iron Furnace
off US 322, 4 miles north of I-76 off
SR 72 on SR 419
Cornwall, PA 17016
(717) 272-9711

Built in 1742 by Peter Grubb, the furnace operated until 1883, producing stoves, kitchenware and farm tools, as well as cannons and ammunition for the Continental Army. Structures include: the original furnace stack, the blast machinery, the blowing tubs, the wagon and blacksmith shops, the open pit mine, the ironmaster's mansion and the Charcoal House.

87. Mercer Museum
Pine and Ashland streets
Doylestown, PA 18901
(215) 345-0210

Exhibits trace the pre-industrial history of the nation from colonization to the Civil War. More than 60 crafts and trades are represented by artifacts and implements from the eighteenth and nineteenth centuries.

88. Fort Necessity
National Battlefield
R.D. 2, Box 528
Farmington, PA 15437-9514
(412) 329-5512

Fort Necessity National Battlefield is located 11 miles east of Uniontown, PA, on US 40. The park consists of three detached sections: the main unit, which includes the battlefield, the reconstruct-ed 1754 fort and earthworks, the Mount Washington Tavern and the visitor center; the Braddock Grave unit, one mile west on US 40; and the Jumonville Glen unit, seven miles west along the crest of Chestnut Ridge. The park also contains traces of the Braddock Road, built by Washington and Braddock in 1754-1755.

89. Fort Ligonier
US 30 and SR 711
Ligonier, PA 15658
(412) 238-9701

A reconstruction of the English fort built in 1758. The museum contains interpretive exhibits from the site, two period rooms and collections of decorative arts.

90. Pennsbury Manor
5 miles south on the Delaware River
at 400 Pennsbury Memorial Road
Morrisville, PA 19067
(215) 946-0400

This 43-acre historic site was the country estate of William Penn. The site includes seventeenth and eighteenth century artifacts, the reconstructed manor house (1683), a worker's cottage, a smokehouse, a bake and brew house, an icehouse, a blacksmith shop, a stable and horse shelter, farm animals, and the formal and kitchen gardens.

91. Germantown Historic District
Germantown Convention and
Visitors Bureau
3 Penn Center Plaza, Suite 2020
Philadelphia, PA 19102

Settled by Hollanders in 1683 and a later group of Germans, the old homes of Germantown are distinguished by their Dutch doors and arched cellar windows. Historic homes in the district include Cliveden (1767), Stenton (1730) and the Deshler-Morris House.

92. Jewish Historical Society of Maryland
15 Lloyd Street
Baltimore, MD 21202
(410) 732-6400

The society maintains a public collection of 150,000 documents, photographs and objects relating to the 300-year his-

tory of Judaism in Maryland. The Jewish Heritage Center, located between the Lloyd Street Synagogue (1845) and the B'nai Israel Synagogue (1876), displays exhibits on both local and worldwide Jewish art and history.

93. Maryland Historical Society
201 West Monument Street
at Park Avenue
Baltimore, MD 21201
(410) 685-3750

The historical society maintains the Museum and Library of Maryland History, which includes period rooms of the nineteenth century Enoch Pratt Mansion, the Darnell Young People's Museum and the Radcliff Maritime Museum.

94. Historic St. Mary's City
SR 5
St. Mary's City, MD 20686
(301) 862-0990 / 862-0960
(800) SMC-1634

This 800-acre outdoor museum complex illustrates the history of St. Mary's City, beginning with the first colonists' arrival on the Ark and the Dove in 1634. Major exhibits include the Godiah Spray Tobacco Plantation, a working reconstruction of a seventeenth century tobacco plantation; Governor's Field, which contains restored, reconstructed and archeological buildings and sites; the Maryland Dove, a replica of the original ship; and an Indian longhouse.

95. The Smithsonian Institution
Constitution Avenue
Washington, DC 20560
(202) 357-2700

The Smithsonian is "the nation's attic" and has numerous museums and galleries, including one in Maryland and two in New York. The complex in Washington, DC, includes art galleries, museums and research facilities.

The National Museum of American History celebrates American culture and innovations. It exhibits the scientific, cultural, technological and political development of the United States.

Within the museum, the first floor focuses upon science and technology; the second floor upon social and political history; and the third upon money, printing and the graphic arts, musical instruments and the history of the armed forces.

Other Smithsonian facilities in the nation's capital are the Anacostia Museum, the Arthur M. Sackler Gallery, the Arts and Industries Building, the Freer Gallery of Art, the Hirshhorn Museum and Sculpture Garden, the John F. Kennedy Center for the Performing Arts, the National Air and Space Museum, the National Gallery of Art, the National Museum of African Art, the National Gallery of Art, the National Museum of American Art, the National Museum of Natural History, the National Portrait Gallery, the National Postal Museum, the National Zoological Park, the Renwick Gallery and the Smithsonian Institution Building (The Castle).

96. Delaware Agricultural Museum and Village
2 miles north of Dover at Junction US 13 and US 13 Alt.
Dover, DE 19901
(302) 734-1618

The exhibition hall features tractors, horse-drawn equipment and dairy and poultry farming objects dating from 1670 to the 1950s. The buildings date from the Civil War era to about 1900, including a one-room schoolhouse, a sawmill, a barbershop, a train station, a farmhouse, a general store, and blacksmith and wheelwright shops.

97. Hall of Records
Legislative Avenue
at Duke of York Street
Dover, DE 19901
(302) 739-5314
The Hall of Records preserves the public archives of Delaware. Included among the historic documents on display is the original charter of 1682 from King Charles II and William Penn's order for the platting of Dover.

98. John Dickinson Plantation
6 miles south of Dover on US 113, then 1/8 mile east on Kitts Hummock Road
Dover, DE 19901
(302) 739-3277

The 1740s brick house and reconstructed farm complex are an example of eighteenth century plantations of the area. This was the boyhood home of John Dickinson, known as "the Penman of the American Revolution" because of his written contributions to the colonial cause.

99. Amstel House
Fourth and Delaware streets
New Castle, DE 19720
(302) 322-2794

The 1730s home is maintained as a museum and was formerly the home of colonial Dutch Governor Van Dyke. It is filled with colonial furniture and household equipment.

100. Dutch House
32 East Third Street
New Castle, DE 19720
(302) 322-2794

This house was built in the late seventeenth century and is believed to be the oldest brick house in the state. It has been restored as a museum and features decorative arts and historical artifacts.

101. The Green
Delaware Street
between Third and Market streets
New Castle, DE 19720

Laid out by Peter Stuyvesant in 1655, The Green and Market Square were the sites of fairs and weekly markets until the early nineteenth century. Also on the Green are a US arsenal (1809) and the New Castle Academy (1798).

102. New Castle Court House
211 Delaware Street
(between Market and Third streets)
New Castle, DE 19720
(302) 323-4453 or (800) 441-8846

The courthouse, built in 1732, has been restored to its 1804 appearance. Flags of the Netherlands, Sweden, England and the United States are displayed on the balcony, showing the ownership of the town by each of these countries during its history. A window in the courtroom floor reveals the remains of the 1689 courthouse.

103. Old Presbyterian Church
25 East Second Street
New Castle, DE 19720
(302) 328-3279

Built in 1707, the Old Presbyterian Church is believed to be the direct successor to the original Dutch Reformed Church of 1657. Graves in the church's cemetery date back to the early eighteenth century.

104. Holy Trinity (Old Swedes) Church
606 Church Street
Wilmington, DE 19801
(302) 652-5629

The oldest active Protestant church in North America, the Holy Trinity Church was built in 1698.

105. *Kalmar Nyckel* Foundation
1124 East Seventh Street at Swede's Landing
Wilmington, DE 19801
(302) 429-7447

Guided tours of the shipbuilding facilities are provided. In 1638, the Swedish ship *Kalmar Nyckel* sailed to Delaware, establishing the state's first permanent colony. A replica of the ship is being constructed, and paintings of the original ship are displayed.

106. Winterthur Museum, Garden and Library
6 miles northwest of the city on SR 52
Wilmington, DE 19735
(302) 888-4600 or (800) 448-3883
TDD (302) 888-4907

This is the largest collection of decorative arts made or used in America from 1640 to 1860. The history and development of early American decorative arts are explored, focusing on social customs, techniques, symbolism and style.

107. The Alexandria Black History Resource Center
638 North Alfred Street
Alexandria, VA 22314
(703) 838-4356

The Resource Center interprets the contributions of African Americans to Alexandria's history and culture from 1749 to the present.

108. Alexandria Convention and Visitors Bureau
The Ramsay House Visitor Center
221 King Street
Alexandria, VA 22314
(703) 838-4200

This building, the oldest in Alexandria, was moved to its present site in 1749 by William Ramsay. The center offers information on historic Alexandria, an orientation videotape, walking tour brochures and guide books.

109. Doorways to Old Virginia
Ramsay House
221 King Street
Alexandria, VA 22314
(703) 548-0100

A guided walking tour of Old Town Alexandria, the tour covers six blocks of the historic seaport. Guides in eighteenth century dress describe the histories of many eighteenth and nineteenth century homes.

110. Fredericksburg Area Museum and Cultural Center
907 Princess Anne Street
Fredericksburg, VA 22401
(703) 371-5668

The museum building was once the town hall and market, where not only goods but political ideas were exchanged. It houses collections of photographs, tools, furniture, paintings, toys and other items that trace the history of Fredericksburg, founded in 1727, as well as the surrounding area.

111. Hugh Mercer Apothecary Shop
Caroline and Amelia Streets
Fredericksburg, VA 22401
(703) 373-3362

Opened in 1761, the apothecary features a drug room with curious bottles, ancient showcases and yellowed ledgers; a sitting room; and a small library used by George Washington as an office.
Demonstrations of eighteenth century medical practices include leeching, cupping, bleeding and herbal remedies.

112. St. George's Church
Princess Anne and George streets
Fredericksburg, VA 22401
(703) 373-4133

This Episcopal church was built in 1732, and the current building dates from 1849. It contains three original L.C. Tiffany windows and a memorial window to Mary Washington. Buried in the churchyard are William Paul, the brother of John Paul Jones, and John Dandridge of New Kent, the father of Martha Washington.

113. St. Paul's Church
St. Paul Boulevard and
City Hall Avenue
Norfolk, VA 23510
(804) 627-4353

Built in 1739 upon the site of a 1641 church known as "the Chapel of Ease," St. Paul's Episcopalian Church was the only building left after the burning of Norfolk in 1776. A cannonball fired from a British ship remains imbedded in its wall. Graves in the cemetery date from the seventeenth century.

114. Beth Ahabah Museum & Archives Trust
1109 West Franklin Street
Richmond, VA 23220
(804) 353-2558

Virginia's only Jewish history museum is descended from one of the oldest Jewish congregations in America. The museum features changing exhibits of documents, historical photographs and religious objects. The archive collection may be used for genealogical research.

115. St. John's Episcopal Church
24th and Broad streets
Richmond, VA 23223
(804) 648-5015

Built in 1741, this is the site where Patrick Henry made his stirring speech in favor of independence.

116. George Washington Birthplace National Monument
RR 1, Box 717
Washington's Birthplace, VA 22443
(804) 224-1732

The monument is located on the Potomac River, 38 miles east of Fredericksburg, VA, and is accessible via Va. 3 and Va. 204. The site itself is a recreation of the eighteenth century Popes Creek Plantation. Park facilities include the historic birthplace home area, colonial farm, burial ground, hiking trails, beach and picnic area.

117. Colonial Williamsburg Historic Area
Colonial Williamsburg Foundation
Box 1776
Williamsburg, VA 23187
(800) 447-8679

With over 100 buildings, this mile long historic area recreates the vitality and historic importance of eighteenth century Williamsburg. Restored buildings in the area include: the Brush-Everard House (1717), the Bruton Parish Church (1712), the Capitol (rebuilt to its 1705 appearance), the Courthouse of 1770, the Governor's Palace (1722), the Public Gaol (1704), the Raleigh Tavern (built before 1742), and the Historic Trades Shops.

118. Colonial National Historical Park: Jamestown and Yorktown
P.O. Box 210
Yorktown, VA 23690
(804) 898-3400

Jamestown and Yorktown, located on the Virginia Peninsula between the James and York rivers, are two of the most important places in colonial American history.
Thanks to the Colonial Parkway, it is easy to follow the sequence of history, from the colonial beginnings at Jamestown in 1607 to the winning of national independence after the decisive Battle of Yorktown in 1781.

119. Bath State Historic Park
Bath, NC 27808

Founded in 1705, Bath is North Carolina's oldest incorporated town. A visitor center offers guided tours of the town, including the restored Palmer-Marsh House (1744) and the Bonner House (1825).

120. Historic Edenton
Visitor Center
108 North Broad Street
Edenton, NC 27932
(919) 482-2637

Edenton was the center of North Carolina's colonial life. Tours of the historic district begin at the visitor center, a late 19th-century frame house. Included in the tour are the Chowan County Courthouse (1767), the Cupola House (1758), the James Iredell House State Historic Site (1773) and the restored St. Paul's Church (1736-1766).

121. Fort Raleigh National Historic Site Cape Hatteras National Seashore
Route 1, Box 675
Manteo, NC 27954

The Fort Raleigh National Historic Site features reconstructions, exhibits, live drama and talks by park interpreters, giving visitors an understanding of the people who backed the colony from the safety of England and the colonists who lived and died here.
The site is located on US 64-264, 3 miles north of Manteo, NC, 92 miles southeast of Elizabeth City, NC.

122. Beaufort Historic District
Beaufort Chamber of Commerce
Box 910
Beaufort, SC 29901

Chartered in 1711, Beaufort is the second oldest town in the state. The historic district features the Beaufort Museum, housed in a 1795 arsenal, and St. Helena's Episcopal Church (1724).

123. Georgetown Historic District
Georgetown Chamber of Commerce
Box 1776
Georgetown, SC 29442

Historic buildings include the Prince George Winyah Church, built in 1737 with brick imported from England, and the Kaminski House, a typical country mansion, furnished with antiques dating from the fifteenth century.

124. Fort Frederica National Monument
Route 9, Box 286-C
St. Simons Island, GA 31522

The park is on St. Simons Island, which is located 12 miles from Brunswick, GA and can be reached via US 17 and the Brunswick-St. Simons (FJ Torras) Causeway. The fort was established in 1736 by James Oglethorpe as a base for military operations against the Spanish in Florida.

125. Fort King George State Historic Site
PO Box 711
Darien, GA 31305
(912) 437-4770

As the the first British outpost in Georgia, from 1721 to 1736, it protected the Altamaha River and its inner passage from French and Spanish attacks.

126. Fort Matanzas National Monument
Visitor Information Center
10 Castillo Drive
St. Augustine, FL 32084
(904) 471-0116

The national monument includes the northern third of Rattlesnake Island and the southern tip of Anastasia Island. A ferry carries visitors to Fort Matanzas, which was built between 1740 to 1742, and is located on Rattlesnake Island, off SR A1A, 14 miles south of St. Augustine. Anastasia Island's visitor center contains exhibits relating the fort's history.

127. St. Augustine's Restored Spanish Quarter
Triay House
29 St. George Street
St. Augustine, FL 32084
(904) 825-6830

The area consists of restored and reconstructed buildings illustrating Spanish colonial life. Guides in period costumes demonstrate 1740s crafts and lifestyles. Some of the buildings include: la Casa de Gallegos (1750s), la Casa de Gómez (1750s), the DeHita/González Houses and the Spanish Military Hospital.

Please note: While we have made every effort to insure the accuracy of the information in this section, certain data such as, but not limited to, phone numbers and mailing addresses, is subject to change. It is always best to plan your visit well in advance and to call ahead for hours and availability.

77

INDEX